Jake Built A Fire In The Fireplace And Then Sat Beside Caitlin. Close.

Handing her drink to her, he brushed her hand lightly. The physical contact, while so slight, burned. Soft, warm skin. A startling awareness that increased his desire.

She smiled at him. "Thank you. We're having quite a storm. There won't be any going home the way I came. This kind of downpour gets the river spilling out of its banks."

She slanted him a look that was hot. He wondered if it was deliberate. Maybe he shouldn't be so hasty in getting rid of her.

While he had no intention of selling any part of the Santerre ranch back to her, how far would she go to try to convince him to do so?

"We have plenty of room," he said in a husky voice. "You can stay all night."

Dear Reader,

Our lives are interwoven with our families and as the years pass, no one can predict outcomes. Falling in love involves two people, but their relationship is also affected by the influence of family, which I like to include in my stories.

Family has always been important in my life, and it is consequential in my books. Readers of *Texas Tycoon's Christmas Fiancée* have met the three men who bonded as kids because of their manipulative fathers. This time it is the world of Jake Benton, a cowboy CEO, a multimillionaire mogul who loves his West Texas cattle ranch and a cowboy's life. Making a bet with his three best friends that he can resist marriage the longest, even if it means getting disinherited, he never expects to cross paths with his beautiful neighbor. Their sizzling attraction plays havoc with bitter feelings from generations of feuding between their families.

Against the backgrounds of Dallas, a West Texas ranch and the French Quarter in New Orleans, the family conflicts give the characters tough choices to make. Each has to cope with events from the past. Caitlin's tenderhearted care for others propels her into a tempestuous relationship with Jake. Ultimately, Jake makes a life-changing discovery that he hopes will win Caitlin's heart. Their story begins....

Sara Orwig

SARA ORWIG

TEXAS-SIZED TEMPTATION

Recycling programs
for this product may
not exist in your area.

ISBN-13: 978-0-373-73099-5

TEXAS-SIZED TEMPTATION

Copyright © 2011 by Sara Orwig

SARA ORWIG

lives in Oklahoma. She has a patient husband who will take her on research trips anywhere from big cities to old forts. She is an avid collector of Western history books. With a master's degree in English, Sara has written historical romance, mainstream fiction and contemporary romance. Books are beloved treasures that take Sara to magical worlds, and she loves both reading and writing them.

To David, Susan, Jim, Hannah, Ellen,
Rachel, Dixie, Joe, Kristine, Cameron, Anne, Brian,
Colin, Elisabeth, Myles. With many thanks to Maureen.

One

Unless the event had been an act of God, when was the last time a life-changing decision had been taken out of his control? Not for years. And he intended to keep it that way.

Beneath darkening skies in the early October afternoon, Jake Benton drove from the private airstrip toward his ranch. From the moment he had left Dallas for the weekend, he had been happy to put distance between himself and his father, who still meddled in his life. They had once fought over which university Jake would attend; later whether he would work in the family business or not. That had brought the first threat to disinherit him. Now when his dad threatened to disinherit Jake, it was over bigger and more important things. Like the most recent demand to get married within the year.

Jake shoved thoughts about his quarrel with his father out of mind. He was on his way to his sprawling West Texas ranch, a retreat where he could get away to relax. The only people for miles were ones who worked for him and his brother. As always when he returned to the ranch, he wondered why he didn't come more often.

He couldn't escape the phone or demands of business, but he could cut back on them.

Jake felt himself relax as the family ranch home that was now his, with its guesthouses, bunkhouse, staff homes, outbuildings, barns, shop, gym and various other structures, appeared in the distance. Irrigated, landscaped yards with beds of brightly colored fall blooms surrounded each house. Jake took in the view, his pleasure over being at the ranch increasing. While clouds hid the sun and thunder rumbled closer at hand, the road divided. Jake took the curve leading to his house. As he turned the corner and drove to the side of the house, he saw someone on his porch. Startled, he stared in surprise. He had a fence and security at the gate leading from the highway. In all the years he had never had any uninvited visitors—until now.

His first reaction was annoyance that someone had breached his privacy and trespassed. Curiosity replaced aggravation. His trespasser, from a distance, looked like a woman. The closer he approached, the more he could see that she was good-looking.

As he pulled to a stop only yards from his house, his gaze raked over her. She stood, walked to the steps and halted to watch him.

Auburn hair piled on her head framed an oval face with prominent cheekbones. Her long legs, encased in pale, slim jeans above Western boots caught his attention. A short leather jacket was cut high, revealing her tiny waist. He was close enough now to experience a skip in his heartbeat.

His last shred of animosity vanished. Searching his memory for a clue to her identity or reason for her on his porch, he remained at a loss. He couldn't imagine why she was waiting for him or how she had known he was coming. Intrigued, determined to get answers, he stepped out of the car.

As his gaze locked with hers, he was startled by a sizzling current of attraction. The chemistry was instant, hot and inviting.

Whatever she was up to, she was audacious. As he approached her, he felt a defiance coming from her that puzzled him.

"Welcome home, Jake," she said in a mellow, quiet voice. In spite of the polite greeting, his sense of a silent challenge increased.

With his gaze still fastened on hers, he climbed the porch steps until he reached the top. Standing only inches from her, he had intended to intimidate her. Instead, he felt ensnared in huge, crystal-green eyes fringed with sweeping auburn lashes. She was gorgeous and he couldn't pull his gaze away.

"I don't often get surprised, but I am now," he admitted. "How'd you get past my security at the gate?"

When a faint smile lifted the corner of her mouth, his attention shifted lower to her full lips. Her mouth made him wonder how it would be to kiss her. Taking a deep breath, he tried to get his thoughts back to his question.

"You don't know me, do you?" she asked.

"No," he admitted. Even more disturbing, she thought he should know her. He never could have gone out with her without remembering. A woman with fabulous looks was not to be forgotten. "You have the advantage. I suspect I should know you. One thing, we've never gone out together," he said, voicing aloud his thoughts.

Another faint smile tugged at her mouth. "No, we haven't," she said patiently. "And to answer your question, I didn't pass your security checkpoint. I came across your ranch from the west."

"There's no gate or road from the west," he said, glancing

beyond her at the land that vanished in a long grove of thick oaks he'd had planted as a windbreak. He could picture beyond the oaks, the flat, mesquite-covered land extending miles to his western boundary. "If you forded the river, it must be mostly dried up now, but rain is threatening," he said, taking a deep breath and smelling the rain that approached. "If you have a vehicle parked in the woods, I better let my foreman know before he calls the sheriff. You're trespassing, which could cause you trouble. I can call the sheriff to have you arrested. I have signs posted."

"This is a desperate effort to talk to you. I haven't been able to get past the secretaries and your attorneys."

His curiosity returned. With an effort he stopped staring at her, focusing instead on who she was. For all he knew, she could be a threat, although at the moment, he would relish a physical struggle with her because he would like to touch her.

An intriguing scent tempted him.

"All right, you want to talk. We can sit here on the porch and have a discussion," he said, motioning toward chairs. He was reluctant to invite her into his house. It crossed his mind that she might be armed. "First though, I'll admit, I don't know who you are."

He received another flicker of amusement. "Caitlin Santerre."

The name was a knife stab. As if ice water had poured over him, he cooled toward her while he stared at her, reconciling his memory of Caitlin Santerre with the beautiful woman standing before him.

"Son-of-a-gun," he said beneath his breath, for once not hiding his reaction to a shock. "You grew up. What the hell do you want with me?"

"You actually don't even know, do you?" she asked, anger

creeping into her tone. "You own our land. I want to buy part of it back."

"You get to the point. Yes, I own it. It's my land since your brother sold it. I was surprised he was willing to sell it to me."

"Will loves money more than maintaining an old family feud, remaining loyal to the family and keeping the home place. All Will wants is to take care of Will," she said.

"I have to agree, but I'm biased. You should have told him to not sell," Jake said, trying to remember the age difference. He had never paid attention to her as a child when he saw her in town. She had seemed years younger and he hadn't given her a thought then or since.

"My brother and I aren't close. We never have been."

"That I can understand," Jake said, a cynical note creeping into his voice when he thought about Will Santerre whom he despised. The litany ran through his thoughts—the first Benton to settle in Texas in the mid-1800s, killing the first Santerre who was trying to divert water. The retaliations followed, which included killing cattle, poisoning water. In the next generation a Santerre son burned the Benton house and barn. The feud continued until his father put Caitlin's father in the hospital after a fistfight. Finally, his generation with the ultimate and most personal clash, made Jake feel the old hurts like a scar. He would always be certain Will Santerre had killed his older sister, Brittany. Will was tried and found not guilty. Will had sworn it was Brittany who caused the car crash, but Jake would never be convinced. His family was guilty of doing things to the Santerres, but his family had always felt justified. While Jake had hated it, Brittany had been in love with Will. Brittany had been Football Queen, Class President, beautiful, popular—Will loved the girls and went after her. Maybe out of both revenge and really wanting her. Maybe just because he had thought she would be a conquest that would make him look good. Jake could never believe anyone as selfish as Will could love another person. As far as he was concerned, Will loved himself more than anybody else. Jake looked at Caitlin. Her beauty now was tempered by the knowledge of her lineage.

The first huge drops of rain fell, slanting to hit along the edge of the porch. "This rain was a twenty-percent chance—most unlikely from the morning weather report. I'll make this short," she said.

"Let me call my foreman about your vehicle—what did you drive?"

She flashed a smile that made Jake forget his hostility again. Her white teeth were even and her smile was a warm invitation as if she were on the verge of sharing a delightful secret. "There's no vehicle. And there's no road," she answered, jerking her head toward the trees. "I came from the west on horseback. He jumped your fence. You might want to tell your foreman I have a tethered horse. I would appreciate getting my horse out of the weather."

"Ah, now I know why no one spotted you. I have men who drive the boundaries, but they can't cover this big ranch all the time. The likelihood of anyone coming across the ranch from any direction other than the highway is minimal to nonexistent. I'm not here most of the time, keep a low profile when I am home, and it's peaceful out here. I don't have enemies—or at least not many," he said, thinking of his former neighbors. Jake glanced at the trees again. "I'll tell someone to bring your horse in so it's sheltered."

"Thanks."

As Jake made his call, more drops fell. He put away his phone. "My foreman will put your horse in the stable closest to the house."

"Thanks."

"This may only be a fall shower. Let's go inside where we

can talk in more comfortable surroundings," Jake suggested, intrigued by her in spite of his burning hatred of her half brother. "Since our grandfathers' days, we haven't had to worry much about trespassers."

"I guess our fathers were less into tearing down fences and stealing livestock from each other than the generations before them. The feud between our families began with the first two men who settled here."

"It may be less violent, but it hasn't ever ended," Jake said, thinking again of Will.

"Where is Will now?"

"He won't ever be back. He's bought a home in San Francisco and also owns a home in Paris. He's into investments. Beyond that, I know little about him. We have virtually no contact."

Knowing they were getting on a bad topic, Jake held the door for her. "This is a turn in the feud—you're the first Santerre to be invited in."

She barely looked at her surroundings as they walked down the wide hall. "So this is where you grew up."

"Yes. The original part of this house is as old as the house where you grew up. I know your dad's house was built later."

"My dad's house no longer exists," she said sharply. "Your crew began demolition last week. It doesn't take long to destroy a structure. Fortunately, Grandmother's house is the one that dates back to the beginning."

Holding back a retort, Jake directed her into a room. "Let's sit in the study," he said.

They entered one of Jake's favorite places, spacious with floor-to-ceiling bookshelves on two walls while the remaining walls were glass. French doors opened onto the wraparound porch and patio, which had been remodeled with an extended roof and comfortable living areas. Beyond the patio, steps led down to a pool with a waterfall, a cabana, chairs and chaise longues. Tropical plants added an appealing touch.

"Have a seat," Jake said. He turned as she sat in a leather wingback chair. In a sweeping glance he took in her blue Western shirt that clung to lush curves and tucked into her snug jeans. Her belt circled a waist that was as small as he had guessed at his first glimpse. The little Santerre kid he had always ignored had turned into a stunning woman. He sat in another leather chair that faced her across a low mahogany table.

She crossed her long legs and he wondered how she would look in a dress. The image made his blood heat. She looked poised, comfortable, unlike someone desperate to get him to agree to something. She also looked desirable. Even though she was a Santerre, there was a red-hot chemistry about her that tempted him to forget who she was.

When he looked up from her legs, his eyes met hers and he was again ensnared. Attraction was tangible. She had to feel it because she held his gaze as invisible sparks heated him. He wanted to know her better. At the same time, the lifelong hatred of all Santerres coated the magnetism with bitterness. Caitlin was as forbidden as poison, yet he wanted to place his lips on her to taste and kiss.

Taking a deep breath he tore his gaze away to return his attention with more composure.

"Have you been waiting long?" he asked. "I took my time flying in here this morning."

"I was willing to wait," she said.

"How'd you know I was coming today?"

Amusement flashed in her expressive eyes. "I've hired a private detective to learn your whereabouts so I could find an opportunity to talk to you. You rarely have a bodyguard with you."

"You're taking a chance because you know I can have you arrested."

"It would be a little more difficult to consider me a trespasser now that you've invited me into your house."

"So you want to buy back part of your ranch. Why didn't you discuss this with your brother?"

"My half brother never gave me the opportunity. It's general knowledge in these parts that traditionally in the Santerre family, the oldest son inherits the ranch. They are raised to protect the ranch, maintain it, keep it in the family. Well, all of that instruction didn't take with Will. He does as he pleases and he has no interest in cowboys, the country or ranch life."

"He told me he didn't," Jake said, thinking about the closing that he hadn't planned to attend and then did just to face Will when he bought out the Santerres. In spite of Will being happy over the sale, the buyout had been sweet revenge—a goal through generations of Bentons to see the last of the Santerres in the area. Jake's attorneys had already informed him that Caitlin wasn't included in the ranch inheritance. Also, she hadn't lived at the ranch since she had graduated from college. He still had thought of her as a child, so he had dismissed her from mind.

"Why didn't Will sell part of the ranch to you since you want it badly?"

"He didn't bother to contact me, either about selling or to ask if I wanted to buy any part of it. Will and I aren't close. He cares only about himself."

"I'd agree with that," Jake stated, remembering the antagonism he had felt toward Will at the closing. Each time he had looked into Will's hazel eyes, he could see loathing mirrored there.

"If it were left up to Will," Caitlin continued, "I would be excluded from the family. Our father felt the same."

"If I remember correctly, your grandmother raised you. She was a Santerre, actually, your father's mother."

"Yes, but unlike him in so many ways. I loved her deeply and she was good to me. Because of her, I'm recognized as a Santerre by everyone except Will."

Jake recalled lots of gossip regarding the Santerre family history—how Caitlin's mother had been a maid for the Santerres, the brief affair...and the resulting baby. And how the baby had been unacknowledged and cut off by Titus Santerre, yet adopted and raised by her paternal grandmother. How Titus Santerre had remained married to Will's mother until her death and did not remarry.

"Why do you want to buy any of the ranch back?" he asked. "You don't live here any longer and you're not a rancher." His gaze drifted over her thick auburn hair that was pinned loosely on her head with a few escaping strands. Looking silky, her hair was another temptation, making him think of running his fingers through the soft strands.

"I adored my grandmother and I loved growing up in her house. The people who worked for her closely were included in her will. Our foreman, Kirby Lenox, Altheda Perkins, who was our cook and now also cleans, and Cecilia Mayes, Grandmother's companion—they all stayed on. Kirby and two who work for him, still run the ranch. They care for the horses and the few cattle we have. Altheda maintains the house, cooking and overseeing the cleaning. Cecilia is elderly now. She devoted her life to Grandmother, first as her personal secretary and later as companion.

"I knew people were still staying there."

"As owner, you could have evicted them."

"I'm not in a rush. I figured they would leave before long. If they didn't, then I planned to tell them they had to go. It is my property."

"I love all of them because they were there when I grew

up. I wanted to keep the house, barn and animals for them as long as they live. I wanted to be able to return occasionally to the ranch house—just as you must do here."

Jake nodded. "Why didn't you tell Will?"

She looked away but he had seen the coldness in her expression that came with his question. "I did tell Will. He just laughed at me and reminded me that my father barely acknowledged my existence so I had no say in what he did with the ranch. He said he would tell me if it looked as if I could come up with more money to buy it and make a better offer than anyone else who bid on it. When the time came, he didn't. I knew nothing about the sale. He didn't legally have to notify me because I had no more part of ownership of the ranch than a stranger."

Jake felt no stir of sympathy for her. Even though she and Will were alienated, Jake couldn't forget that they were both Santerres. The same blood ran in her veins as in Will's.

"You know I can't work up much sympathy for a Santerre," Jake admitted, voicing his thoughts aloud. "Not even a beautiful one."

One dark eyebrow arched as she gave him a level look. "You're honest. I'm not asking you to like me or even see me again in your lifetime. I just want to buy the house and part of the land. Grandmother never owned it. There was a stipulation in my father's will assuring her she could live there the rest of her life and then it would belong to Will. All I want is a small part."

"What advantage for me would there be in doing any such thing?" he asked. "It would mean keeping a Santerre for a neighbor. You surely heard the family histories and know what kind of past we've had."

"Oh, I've heard," she replied lightly as if discussing the weather. "The first Benton killed the first Santerre over water. The river meanders and thus the argument continues about each family's rights and boundary. Our great-great-grandfathers were political opponents. Your family supposedly burned down our barn in the early days, rustled cattle, stole our horses. The list is long."

"You've left out the most recent episode that touched our lives, at least it affected mine. You may have been young enough to miss it. I'm thirty-four. You must be about twenty-two."

Her eyes danced with amusement. "You're a little off. If that were the case, when you were seventeen in high school, I would have been toddling off to kindergarten. No, I'm twenty-eight now."

Smiling, he shrugged. "You were a little kid. You might as well have been five when I was seventeen. I paid no attention to you at that age."

"Mmm, I'll have to remedy that. I have no intention of letting you continue to ignore me," she drawled, making his heart skip because she was flirting with him.

"Maybe I'll have to reassess my attitude toward Santerres," he said.

"You might be surprised by what you'd find," she rejoined, slanting him a coy smile that made his pulse jump.

"You should make me forget you're related to Will. As far as our family is concerned, Will caused my sister Brittany's death."

"When the District Attorney pressed charges and Will was brought to trial, he was found innocent. The car wreck was ruled an accident. Will has been cleared of that charge," Caitlin stated matter-of-factly.

"I'll never feel he was innocent," Jake replied. "Will testified that Brittany tried to run him off the road. But she was in love with him. Will is the one who ran her off the road."

"The jury found Will innocent. Will and I barely speak.

He'll probably cease to do so now that our father is gone. Although, my success in my profession has given Will a grudging mellowing toward me. Not enough to inform me of his decision to sell the ranch, much less of the agreement to sell it to you."

"Will is rotten," Jake said, thinking more about Caitlin's silky auburn hair and huge eyes, still amazed to learn her identity.

"Please think about this. I want to save the house and people's livelihoods that you'll take away. I love them and they're older now. I feel responsible for their well-being because they've devoted their lives to my grandmother and to me."

"Noble, but they also got paid to do so and probably a damned good salary."

"Sure, but it went beyond that. That house holds happy memories. Please rethink my request to buy before you answer hastily."

He smiled at her as he sat in silence and studied her. "All right, I'll think about it, but I doubt if I'll change my mind."

"If so, your decision has to be spite." Her expression didn't change. Green eyes observed him coolly. "You have one of the largest ranches in the state as it is and now you've bought up neighboring ranches as well as ours. I urge you to have an open mind when you give this thought."

"It isn't spite. At least not toward you. It's vengeful where Will is concerned. I was delighted to buy him out. Even happier to tear down Will's home place, turning it into rubble that will be cleared. Eventually, in its place will be mesquite, cactus and bare ground."

Lightning crackled and popped while thunder made the windows rattle. Rain began to drum against the house.

Jake's mind raced as his gaze roamed over her again. Her beauty pulled on his senses and there was an unmistakable physical attraction, but he didn't care to pursue it. She was a Santerre and he wasn't selling land back to her. She should have talked to Will immediately after their father's death about her wishes to keep their grandmother's property. He glanced beyond her through the French doors at the downpour, listening to the loud hiss of rain.

He glanced at his watch; it was almost six o'clock. He wanted her to stay for dinner when common sense said to get rid of her. Tell her no, get her out of his life and keep the property. She would give up and go on with her life if she learned there was no hope of regaining her childhood home.

But, traitorous or not, he was enjoying the sight of her too much. "You might as well stay for dinner. You can't ride home in this and I don't care to get out in it right now. It's a gully washer and you know as well as I do how fast creeks and streams here will flood, so just stay. I can take you home later and you can get your horse when it's convenient."

She gave him another of her long, assessing looks and he couldn't guess what ran through her thoughts. "Very well, thank you."

He nodded. "This place is stocked. All the staff is gone, Their work is minimal since I'm here so little. I give them notice when I want them. My cook lives here on the ranch, and the other house staff live in town. Since you're here, I'll ask Fred to come in the morning. He lives on the ranch, so it's easy for him to do so. Dinner will be what I can rustle up."

"That's fine. You can keep it simple."

"Want a drink? Wine, soft drink, mixed drink, beer?"

"A glass of water would be great," she said.

"Let's go to the family room. It's more comfortable."

"Fine, lead the way," she said, standing in a fluid motion.

She was tall, although a good six inches shorter than he was. They walked into an adjoining room twice the size of the study with windows and French doors with another, more panoramic view of the storm. French doors also opened onto the porch and the covered patio. She crossed to the windows to look out while he built a fire in a stone fireplace. He went to the bar to get her water and get himself a cold beer.

"We can sit outside and watch the storm if you prefer, although it may be chilly. I can build a fire and I'll cook out there."

"I have a jacket."

"And I don't get cold," he said. They walked out to the patio with its comfortable furniture, stainless-steel equipment and a state-of-the-art cooker.

"Even though there are no walls, you have what amounts to another few rooms out here," she remarked, glancing around at a living area, a kitchen area and the cabana and pool.

"It's livable. A fire will make it more so." He built a fire in a fireplace and then sat facing her near the blazing orange flames.

Handing her drink to her, he brushed her hand lightly. The physical contact, while so slight, burned. Soft warm skin. A startling awareness increased his desire.

She smiled at him. "Thank you. We're having quite a storm. There won't be any going home the way I came. As you said, this kind of downpour gets the river spilling out of its banks."

She slanted him a look that was hot. He wondered if it was deliberate. Maybe he shouldn't be so hasty in getting rid of her after dinner.

While he had no intention of selling any part of the Santerre ranch back to her, how far would she go to try to convince him to do so?

"It's already dark out because of the storm," he said. "We have plenty of room," he added in a husky voice. "You can stay all night."

Two

"A Santerre staying overnight with a Benton. It's a shocking invitation that would turn our relatives topsy-turvy if they had known."

"Scared to stay with a Benton?"

"Not remotely. I look forward to it," she said, smiling at him. "It's just that never in my wildest imaginings would I have guessed I would be here overnight. One Santerre is definitely shocked."

"This is a stormy night, so better to stay inside."

"Good. Staying longer will give me more time to try to talk you into selling. You don't live here year round, why would you want so much more land? I know you've bought the ranch to the east of this one in addition to buying ours."

"The first and foremost reason is oil," he answered. "My brother thinks there may be oil in this general area. You have to know that he's already drilling to the west of your grandmother's house."

"I see the activity with the trucks coming and going all hours. A rig is up now. From the upstairs floors we can see the work. They have fenced off the area so the cattle won't roam there. I don't think you'll find any oil. My dad went through this at one time."

"Gabe thinks there may be oil on your ranch, or on the old Patterson place. That's why I wanted the land to the east, partially why I wanted your home place. Mostly I wanted to buy out Will and see the last of the Santerres in Nealey County. The people who worked for your grandmother are not Santerres. They would eventually have to go, but I haven't been in a rush to run them off."

"I have never done anything to hurt you or your family," she stated quietly, but he saw the flare of fire in her eyes indicating animosity was not his alone.

"No, you haven't. Admit it, though, you don't like me or any other Benton."

She glanced away. "I was raised to feel that way. I'm sure both families are at fault." Her attention returned to him. "Your dislike hinges primarily on your sister and Will, even though Will was found innocent."

Jake hoped he hid the sudden clenching of his insides as the old anger stirred again. She had touched a nerve. "I'll always feel my sister's death was due to Will."

"Even though a jury found him innocent?" Caitlin asked. "From what Will said, your sister was the one at fault."

"My sister had the poor judgment to fall in love with your half brother," Jake said, thinking Caitlin should have left the topic alone because she stirred memories of the most abhorrent event in his life. It was the ultimate culmination of his hatred of Will. "Brittany didn't live to tell her side of the story."

"At the trial Will testified that they had a fight and she drove off in a rage. He said he was afraid she would have a wreck and he followed her. He tried to get in front of her car so he could slow her down. He testified that when he tried to pass her, she sideswiped his car. She lost control and crashed."

"I'll always think Will sideswiped her car. Will was the one who wanted her out of his life. She wanted him to marry her."

"That never came out in the trial, although it was common talk. Will admitted to Grandmother that Brittany wanted him to marry her."

"You know a lot about it."

"I was there, even if I was younger than you."

"She was pregnant with Will's baby," Jake said, feeling the dull hurt that came when he thought about Brittany's crash. "Brittany told me. She was in love with him, too. I'm convinced Will ran her off the road and she crashed," Jake said, hurt growing with each word. He hated having painful memories dredged up again.

Caitlin gasped. "I always figured talk of pregnancy was just a rumor. It was never brought up at the trial."

"My mother didn't know about it. My dad didn't want it brought out at the trial and your family sure as hell didn't," Jake said. "I will always blame Will. I don't believe he told the truth about that night, but no one will ever know because only two people were present. At the time of the trial, one of them was dead," Jake stated, bitterness filling him as he sank into dark memories of a painful time. "We better get off this subject if you want to have a civil conversation with me."

Jake gazed into fiery green eyes. Caitlin made no effort to hide her anger. He could feel the waves of antagonism that revealed her flirting was simply a means to try to get what she wanted from him.

"So that's why you hate Will so much," she said.

"Will and I have competed in school in sports and in the

classroom. I was captain of the football team when he wanted to be. We both were on the baseball team. I had more home runs than Will. He had more stolen bases. I was my class president and the next year he was his class president. We were both on the debate team. Will and I have had plenty of our own battles. I never put Will in the hospital or vice versa."

"You broke his nose. Actually, I wasn't too sorry when I heard that. I thought a good punch was well deserved."

"It definitely was," he said lightly. "It was the loss of Brittany that tops my list of complaints against Will. I loved my sister and I hated to see her go out with Will. Brittany and I fought constantly over that. When she could, she hid her relationship with Will from our dad. I should have told him, but I don't think it would have helped. She was eighteen, a senior. Will was eighteen by then. I was still seventeen. She would have done what she wanted. I don't think anyone could have stopped her. Not even that fatal night."

"As a Benton, you'll always think Will was guilty."

"Yes. While you'll always think he's innocent. We're at an impasse on the issue and it makes even a business deal between us an emotional event that can't be looked at in a purely impartial way."

"Will's no angel and we've never gotten along. Grandmother sat him down and made him tell her what happened. He swore that was the truth and I don't think even Will could have lied to her. She could be a formidable woman. More intimidating than my father."

Jake sipped his beer and listened to the rain, remembering all the emotional upheaval of that time in their lives. He could imagine easily Will Santerre lying to his grandmother. He looked at Caitlin and saw a Santerre, Will's half sister. The ultimate irony would be to seduce her.

He had no intention of selling one inch of the Santerre place back to her.

How valuable was the land to her? Was trying to obtain it worth the price of seduction?

"That's Will," Caitlin continued. "What he did has little to do with me other than the fact that the same blood runs in our veins. There is no love lost between the two of us, so do not lump me with him." The air was thick with hostility again. There was a fine line between them that kept them civil and caused her to flirt with him. He owned her family home and it was headed for destruction. In turn, he was beginning to want her in his bed. The more he was with her, the more he desired her.

She placed her palm on his cheek, startling him. "I told you. I'm going to make you see me as a woman and not as a Santerre."

"I do already," he answered in a husky voice, letting go thoughts about past history. Her hand was warm, soft against his cheek and he wanted her to keep it there. He longed to slip his arm around her waist and pull her into his embrace, to lean close to taste her lips.

Instead, when she sat back in her chair, he took her empty glass from her. "Want something stronger than water this time?"

"I'll have another glass of water," she said, smiling at him and getting up to follow him to the bar. She slid onto a high bar stool and watched as he filled another glass of water and sat on a bar stool facing her.

With their knees lightly touching, the temperature on the patio rose a notch in spite of the rain-chilled air.

"Now what can I do to get you to pay attention to me?" she asked.

He smiled. "You have my full attention right now," he said. "Should it wander, you'll figure out some way to capture my notice again. Some way as clever as getting into my house and spending the evening with me. You managed that easily."

"Right now we're captives of the storm. We both have to be here." She leaned forward, her face closer to his. "I don't know whether I can ever get you to see me apart from my family."

"I promise you," he replied in a huskier voice, "that I see you as Caitlin, a beautiful woman."

Something flickered in the depths of her eyes and she got a sensual, solemn expression that made his heartbeat race. As his gaze dropped to her mouth, his desire to kiss her grew. He wondered about her kiss, resolving to satisfy his curiosity before the night was out.

"Now we have the whole evening to get to know each other. Do you work, Caitlin?"

She nodded. "I'm a professional photographer."

"You must be good if you're earning a living at it."

Swirling her glass of water, she replied, "I freelance and I do earn a living at it."

One dark eyebrow arched. "Why do you want to stay out here when you have a busy life elsewhere in the world?"

"Same reason you're here, probably," she replied. "I can relax, get away from everything else and have solitude."

He sipped his drink and nodded. "You're right," he admitted. "This is an escape for me."

"What do you need to escape from? Business decisions? Women?"

He laughed. "Never women."

"You think about it—I'll make a nice neighbor and the old feud will die with us. I won't fight with you over the boundary, over water, never over the mineral rights, which I'm certain you won't sell back to me, but that's not my purpose here. I want to keep the home for all those people I told you about. Selfishly, also for my own memories and pleasure."

She sipped her water and turned to watch the rain that still came in torrents. "We're having a record breaker."

"Maybe it'll be a night to remember," he said softly. She gave him a sultry look. He wondered if she hadn't wanted the ranch from him if she would have been far less friendly. She had a convincing act to get what she wanted.

"It already has been," she replied. He took her chin in hand to hold her face so he could look into her eyes.

"Are you playing with me to get what you want, Caitlin?" he asked.

"Perhaps, but you're doing the same thing."

"I didn't come to the ranch wanting something from you."

"You do now," she replied, and his heart drummed. He wanted to close the last few inches between them to kiss her. As if she guessed his intent, with a deft move, she twisted away from his light grasp and sat back, smiling coyly at him.

"What would it hurt to sell a piece of the ranch back to me? You could still search for oil and reap the rewards if you find it. The little parcel you'd sell to me, you'd really never miss."

"You could turn right around and give it to Will. As a matter of fact, how do I know that he hasn't had a change of heart and sent you to buy a piece of the ranch back for him? If I sell to you, it's yours to do with as you see fit."

"You can write it in the contract. I'll swear in front of a judge if you want—I absolutely am not doing this for Will," she said and her expression frosted. "Will and I speak only when necessary. Our father barely recognized me. Will has snubbed me on the street in town before. There's no love lost between us."

"I'd think you'd be glad to be rid of the house and the land that belonged to your father and that Will inherited. That would be a constant reminder of your status in the family when you're here. And a reminder your grandmother couldn't own the house she lived in. The Santerres were not considerate of the women in the family."

"No. When I'm in the house where I grew up, my blood father and Will are an insignificant part of it. My father and Will were at her house for family get-togethers, rarely any other times. Grandmother couldn't own the land or the house, but she had other assets. She left Will a token $25,000, otherwise all her money, savings, stocks, bonds, went to me. One thing, Will had to mind Grandmother and he hated that. Will never took orders well from anyone except Grandmother and sometimes his father. Grandmother made him mind and it irritated him no end, but she was the one person on this earth Will truly feared. He feared and cooperated with his father just to the point to keep in his good graces. Will's mother spoiled him terribly. She may have contributed greatly to Will being the selfish, self-centered person he is."

"Did you ever go to your father's house?"

She shook her head and stood, watching the rain. "No, except for Christmases when I was young. Later my father and Will would travel to exotic places to celebrate. I think they were both frightened of Grandmother. They didn't mess with her. I haven't seen Will since my father's funeral. We talked on the phone after I learned about the sale of the ranch. That's how I know Will is living in California and Paris. I'm my father's daughter by blood only. Since I didn't grow up with him, he had little influence on my life. Grandmother raised me to think for myself and form my own opinions. I keep telling you, please don't categorize me with Will." Caitlin tilted her head, studying Jake.

"I haven't. I can keep you and Will separate in my mind." Jake reached out to touch a stray lock of her hair. "I have a suggestion. Let's set aside business so we can enjoy the next few hours. For a while, let's forget that I'm a Benton and you're a Santerre. We can get to know each other on another level that doesn't involve the past, but is the present. If we'd just met, we wouldn't be into all this family history. I think we'll have a better evening that we're compelled by rain to share."

She smiled. "You feel compelled to share this evening with me?"

"You've already said we're captive for tonight and I never said the time together was a bad thing. I'm just trying to make it better by removing some of the remnants of the family feud for a few hours. We can always return to swords' points."

She laughed softly. "Deal. At least we can try. We'll see how long it lasts."

"Excellent," he said, smiling at her. Again, there was a flicker in the depths of her eyes and his insides tightened. She was responsive to him, willing to flirt. She wanted to kiss, he was sure of it, but he was determined to wait until the right moment.

"So, Caitlin, tell me about professional photography. Do you have a studio somewhere?"

"Yes, I do in Houston as well as galleries in Houston and in Santa Fe. I have homes both places."

"Impressive."

She smiled as she peered over the edge of her drink at him. "You're not really impressed. I like my work. Actually, I love my work."

"And what kind of photography do you do?"

"Don't sound as if I'm playing marbles for a living," she said, her smile taking the bite out of her words. "I take pictures of people, families, children, celebs, pets. I specialize in black-and-white photography of people and children. I already know about you—the CEO of Benton Energy, Inc.

Your father is retired now and you run the company. Your brother Gabe is CEO of Benton Drilling."

"Right. Before hunger sets in, I'll fire up the grill for steaks. I'll put potatoes in to cook." He went to the refrigerator to remove the steaks and put them on the grill.

While he cooked, she helped him get salads and water on the table. When she was finished, she perched on the bar stool nearest him to talk to him. "This is a wonderful patio. You can sit outside, yet you're protected from the elements here."

"I enjoy it when I'm here," he said, glancing beyond the patio at the pool that was splashing as raindrops hit the blue surface. "No swimming in this weather." Lightning streaked the sky in a brilliant flash. "If the lightning worries you, we can go inside."

"I'm fine."

"So what does worry you, Caitlin?"

"Losing the property, not being able to help the people who worked for Grandmother through the years."

"I walked into that one."

"So what worries you, Jake?"

"Business failure. My dad's interference in my life."

"You're a little old for your daddy to interfere, especially since you're running a large company," she said and he detected the amusement in her voice.

"Oh, no. I have a manipulative father. At least he tries and I resist. It's not quite the same for my brother. Sometimes I think Brittany dated Will out of rebellion against Dad's constant attempt to dominate her life."

She laughed. "That's mind-boggling. You are definitely not the type to have someone try to control you."

He grinned, turning from the steaks to sit near her for a few minutes. "I like your smile, your laughter. When you laugh, it's a sunny spring day."

"Thank you. That's a nice compliment," she replied. "Too bad you're not Jake Smith and I'm not Caitlin Jones. The night might be incredibly different."

"For tonight, we can try to be Jake Smith and Caitlin Jones. We've already agreed to forget business. Just stretch it a little more and pretend we don't have family histories."

"That's a giant stretch with pitfalls all along the pathway, but it would have been nice," she added and sipped her water.

He leaned down so his face was closer to hers and her eyes widened. "Try. You have an imagination. See me as someone you just met," he urged, thinking she had the greenest eyes he had ever seen. Her perfume tormented him and her mouth was a constant temptation.

"While it's an exciting prospect, it's the way to disaster. Impossible," she answered breathlessly and he was certain she felt the attraction, too.

"Coward," he teased with a faint smile, wanting to lean the last few inches and kiss her. She tilted her face up another degree.

"Wicked man," she replied, smiling to make light of her words.

It would be so easy to close the mere inches of distance and kiss her and she wanted the kiss as much as he, but he resisted. He wanted her to be eager to kiss with no hesitation. The tantalizing moments were building his desire. Hopefully, hers, too.

"Your steaks may be crispy now," she remarked.

He hurried to flip the steaks. He turned, catching her studying him. "Now, wine with dinner?" he asked.

"Yes, thank you," she replied and he moved behind the bar to get a bottle of Shiraz.

In a short time they were seated near the fireplace with dinner in front of them. She was a dainty eater, telling him about her gallery in Santa Fe while he mentally peeled away the blue Western shirt. His appetite for steak diminished. To his surprise, he wanted to see her again beyond tonight and he wanted to take her dancing so he could hold her in his arms.

Common sense told him to forget both things. As a Santerre, when they got down to business, she was going to be unhappy with him because he didn't want to leave a Santerre house standing. The people who had worked for her grandmother could retire or find other jobs, he was sure. He would look into hiring them himself.

Out of sentiment Caitlin wanted the house she grew up in, but she spent little time here. She could move everything out of the house into another home elsewhere. He saw no valid reason to sell the place back to her and several reasons to turn her down. He didn't want Santerres left in the county. He didn't want to have to worry about Caitlin and that old house sitting in the center of his property, leaving part of the property out of his control. If Gabe struck oil, it would be even more important to own the land. While he had mineral rights, he didn't want to have to drive around Caitlin's holdings.

Was he being uncooperative because she was a Santerre? So what? It was his property, legally purchased and he couldn't help if her half brother had not informed her about the sale or her father hadn't included her in ownership. From all he'd heard, her father never had involved her in anything in his life. It was solely the grandmother who had adopted Caitlin to give her a Santerre life.

"Your grandmother has been gone now—what—five years?" Jake asked, trying to recall when he heard that Madeline Santerre had passed away.

"Yes. You have an excellent memory because I know that wasn't a date that meant anything to you," Caitlin replied, looking away. "I loved her with all my heart," she added quietly. Her emotional answer indicated she probably cared so much for the people who had worked for her grandmother because she didn't have anyone else. Her father and half brother had rejected her all her life. So had her birth mother in giving her up for adoption. "The minute Grandmother heard my mother planned to put me up for adoption, she stepped up and took me in."

"So where did you go to college, Caitlin?"

"To Texas University and then to Stanford. My degree is from Stanford. I had intended to go into law, but by my junior year I was earning a lot of money with photography, so I finished college and became a photographer. What about you, Jake?"

"Texas University, too, but years ahead of you. Then a master's in business from Harvard. Then back to work here. Pretty simple and predictable."

"Sure," she said, smiling at him. "You told me what you don't like, so what do you like, Jake?"

"Beautiful women, slow, hot kisses—"

She laughed, interrupting him. "That was not what I had in mind. Besides women, what do you like?"

He grinned. "Making money and doing business deals, watching the business grow, the usual. I swim, I play golf, play basketball with my friends, I ski, I like snow-covered mountains or tropical islands. I'm easy to please. Your turn."

"I'm even easier to please. I like a riveting book, quiet winter nights, getting just the right picture, little children—"

"That sounds like marriage is looming."

"Not at all. No man in my life, but I hope someday. Don't you want to marry someday?"

"Yes, but not this year," he said a little more forcefully than he had intended.

She laughed. "Okay, so you're not ready. I think I can make the same promise safely. I will not marry this year," she said, mimicking him and he had to smile and was relieved she made light of his comment.

The rain turned to a steady, moderate rain. Jake took her hand, aware of her smooth skin, the warmth and softness of her. "Let's go in where it's warmer. I'm glad we don't have to get out in this," he said.

She looked down at her clothes. "I just have what I'm wearing. If you can stand seeing me in the same thing in the morning, only more wrinkled, I'm happy to stay because water may be over some of the bridges, I'd guess."

"Great." He switched on lights in the living area. The fire had burned low and he added logs.

He put on music and took her hand, pulling her to her feet. "Come here, Caitlin, and let's dance," he said, drawing her to him on the polished oak floor in a space between area rugs.

She came into his arms easily, following his lead. He liked holding her, wanting her more with each hour that passed. Common sense still screamed to keep his distance to avoid entanglement of any kind with her, but it was a losing argument. It would be the ultimate irony to seduce Will's half sister, except Will wouldn't care because he obviously had no fondness or even polite consideration for Caitlin.

Jake tightened his arms around her and moved slowly with her. "This is good, Caitlin," he said quietly, more to himself than her.

"Not wise, but it's good," she added, indicating that she must hold the same view of getting acquainted that he had.

"So you like to dance."

"I love to dance and I'm glad you thought of this," she said softly. They moved quietly, conversation ceasing and he was sorry when the music came to an end.

She looked up at him. He held her lightly in his embrace and he felt as if he were tumbling down into a sea of green, falling headlong without any hope of stopping. He had waited long enough.

Three

Caitlin's heart drummed as she gazed into Jake Benton's eyes. Her afternoon had turned her world topsy-turvy. All her life she had been given reasons to dislike the Bentons. Her grandmother had hated Jake's father for things he had done to her son, Caitlin's father, in the years the men were growing up. They had been thrown together at school as well as in town. Grandmother had disliked Jake because of complaints about him from Will.

During the past month, Caitlin herself had developed hostility toward Jake, which had increased swiftly when she found a stone wall of interference keeping her from contacting him.

He was important, busy, an oil millionaire, but he should have had a streak of common courtesy to at least take a phone call from someone from the neighboring ranch. While the bitterness between the families could have made him unreceptive, she suspected he was never even told that she was trying to contact him.

Growing up, she had disliked the Bentons because she had been taught to. Jake's snubs had added fuel to the fires of contempt. The only way to get the property back from him was to communicate with him. When she had learned he was expected at the West Texas ranch, she had decided to confront him to force him to listen to her request.

He was being as stubborn as she had expected. What she hadn't anticipated was the scalding chemistry the moment they were face-to-face. It was an intense attraction he felt as much as she did. He also probably hated it as much as she did. Except he had seduction in his eyes. She could imagine how much it would amuse him to seduce a Santerre, even one on the fringe of the family. Titus Santerre's illegitimate child whom he only grudgingly acknowledged because his own mother adopted her.

The thoughts swirled briefly and then vanished. Caitlin's gaze locked with Jake's. His blue eyes held a blatant hunger. Her breathing altered while her temperature rose and her heart skipped. She tilted her face up, knowing she should step away and never kiss him, never open a Pandora's box of problems.

The instant attraction had mushroomed with each hour. A kiss might send it soaring out of control. She had no intention of repeating her mother's big mistake in life that had left Caitlin abandoned and hurt.

"Caitlin," Jake said in a quiet, husky voice that conveyed desire and was an invitation to her.

How could she have this intense sexy reaction to him? A man she had disliked her entire life even though she had never known him or talked to him before? *Get away from him,* an inner feeling urged. He was over six feet of danger to her peace of mind. A kiss would only make things worse. There was no way a kiss would have positive results.

"No," she whispered without moving an inch.

He slipped his hand behind her head, cupping her head lightly. "This is something we both want," he whispered, his gaze lowering to her mouth. "I have since we were standing on the porch this afternoon."

Her lips parted, tingled in anticipation. She was lost to his seductive ways and her own desire, the volatile chemistry between them, her own foolishness.

He leaned down, slowly, tantalizingly. His tongue stroked her lower lip and then he brushed her mouth with his own. Electricity streaked as swiftly as a bolt of lightning flashing outside. Her insides knotted while she slid an arm around his neck. She moved as if she were a puppet with someone else pulling the strings.

His arm tightened around her waist, drawing her more tightly against him.

His kiss scalded, teased. Lust burst in her, sending sparks through her being. She wanted him, needing to touch and kiss and make love. Yet the nagging knowledge that she was kissing a Benton persisted for minutes until his kiss demolished her concern.

Her sigh was consumed by his mouth over hers. When he leaned over her, she tightened her arm around his neck, her body molding to his long, hard strength. Her heart drummed as need built. She wanted him to keep kissing her, longed to run her hands over him.

Fireworks burst in her. His spectacular kisses thawed resistance, escalating her longing and response. She pressed against him to hold him tighter, kissing him with all her being, intending to make him melt and give in to her requests. Caution no longer existed.

His tongue stroked hers; she kissed him deeply in return,

slowly thrusting her tongue over his. The faint moans of pleasure were hers. Her hand went to his shirt to twist free top buttons and slip her fingers across his warm, muscled chest.

Running his hands through her hair, he sent pins tumbling and auburn locks falling.

Hot, low inside her, need heightened. She craved him with a hunger that built with each kiss.

Jake's hand slipped down her back to her waist, sliding lightly over her bottom.

His breathing was as ragged as hers and beneath her hand his heartbeat raced. Caressing her nape, he trailed his fingers to her throat, drifting lower lightly down over her breast to her waist.

As he caressed her, the tingling electricity finally sent a warning that broke through her stormy senses. Moving mechanically, she stepped back a fraction to stop their kisses.

"Jake, wait. This is getting out of hand. I never intended this to happen and neither did you."

He framed her face with his hands. "You never expected it to happen when you came to my place. From the moment we faced each other on the porch, we both wanted to kiss. It was inevitable. I still desire you and you still want me to kiss you because it shows in your expression."

With his words her heart raced faster. He was right and it was obvious, but that didn't make it acceptable. He had nothing to lose. She definitely did.

"Okay, so it shows. Common sense tells me to stop. You and I aren't friends. That's a prerequisite to me for someone to be a lover. An extremely close friend."

Her heart raced as she talked and her gaze was held by his that conveyed his desire. She wanted to lean the last few inches and return to his steamy kisses. He was on target totally, but she had some resistance. Reminding herself of her mission and that he was a Benton, she moved away. "I think we should stop dancing and go back to conversation," she said, heading toward a sofa. She turned to glance at him.

He stood watching her. Locks of his brown hair had fallen across his forehead. His tight jeans revealed his desire that hadn't diminished. Even with distance between them, his expression held lust. His gaze roamed slowly over her and his perusal might as well have been a caress.

Tingling, her body sent entirely different signals from what her logic conveyed. Without taking his gaze from hers, he crossed the room to her. Each step closer made her heart flutter faster. He walked up to her, wrapping his arms around her, bending to kiss her. It was a demanding, possessive kiss that seared and made her weak in the knees.

His hand locked behind her head, his fingers tangling in her hair while he kissed her and shattered her resistance. She pressed against him, losing the battle willingly, pouring kisses back while she clung to him with her arm around his neck. Her other hand roamed down his back and then across the strong column of his neck. Her fingers combed through his short, thick hair. She was never going to forget Jake's kisses. The fleeting thought was as unwanted as his kisses *should* have been.

Why did he have such a devastating effect?

She didn't care why or how threatening they were. His kisses made her want more of him, made her respond and moan with pleasure. Kisses that locked in memory as they awakened needs long dormant, exploded longing and imagination.

When his hands began to free the buttons of her shirt, she gathered her wits to take another stand.

"Jake, stop now. I have to." She gasped for air, looking up

at him, fighting the temptation to rake her fingers through his unruly locks to comb them off his forehead.

Giving her a searching look, he released her. "Want a glass of water or anything to drink?" he asked suddenly. When she declined, he turned and left the room.

She didn't know if he had to put distance between them to help them both cool or just wanted a drink. Whatever the reason, she welcomed his absence and was grateful he had left her. While her heart raced, her breathing sounded as if she had just run a race.

Why, oh, why had she found this excitement and magnetism with Jake Benton—literally the worst person she could think of to feel drawn to.

On the other hand, she should seize the moment, take advantage of the heat between them—as he would—and try to win his cooperation about selling to her.

She glanced at the rain that was coming down harder again. She was in for hours more with Jake and she intended to make the most of them without yielding to his seductive lovemaking.

She sat on the sofa, still conscious of the slight brush of their fingers as he joined her to sit near her.

"When do we return to business?" she asked.

"How about next week when I've had time to think about this? You've known you want to buy back the property, but this is all new to me since late afternoon."

"Why do I suspect you're stalling, although I don't know why you would. Maybe the prospect of seduction tonight is keeping you from flinging a refusal at me."

One corner of his mouth lifted slightly. "That's a sufficient enough reason," he said, turning to look into her eyes. Tingling again, she drew a deep breath.

"I don't know why I have this reaction to you," she admitted.

One dark eyebrow arched. "Man, beautiful woman, there it is," he said. "Elemental."

"Not even remotely elemental," she replied. "I hate to admit to you, few men have the effect you've had."

Something flickered in the depths of his eyes and his chest expanded as he drew a deep breath.

"Oh, my, I shouldn't have divulged that to you," she said, her pulse drumming again.

"No, you shouldn't have if you want me to keep my distance. Remarks like that—there's no way in hell I can sit back and say, 'How nice.'" He moved closer. His arm went around her waist and he lifted her to his lap.

Her instant protest ended as his mouth met hers and they kissed again. Her heart pounded while she clung to him, kissing him hungrily. He cradled her against his shoulder, kissing her while his free hand ran over her hip and along her thigh, sliding up to her breast to stroke in slow circles that taunted even through her lacy bra and cotton shirt.

Fiery tingles radiated from his touch. She should have left well enough alone, but the thought was dim and slid away. Desire surged in a scalding heat running in her veins.

His hand slipped down over her stomach, inching lower between her thighs. Even through her heavy jeans, she could feel his touch as if it were fire.

With an effort she sat up. While she gasped for breath, she gripped his wrist to hold his free hand. "You stop. I shouldn't have told you what I did. We've gone too far too fast."

"Not at all," he argued in a husky, gravelly tone.

She slipped off his lap to the other end of the sofa where she turned to face him. His hooded gaze indicated he still wanted her.

"We should get on some safe topic. Tell me about your hobbies. Your brother and your parents. Your controlling father that meddles in your life."

"My father is the last thing I want to discuss or even think about tonight. I've been enjoying the evening beyond the obvious frustrations. I do not need to drag anger back into my life." He stood. "I'm getting a beer. Want something else? Soft drink? How about homemade lemonade? Juice, milk, wine, martini, any mixed drink—whatever you like?"

"I'll have that lemonade, please, which sounds absolutely wonderful."

"I won't tell you what sounds absolutely wonderful to me," he said, his suggestive drawl conveying a double entendre that was as sizzling as his touch.

"Stop that, Jake. No flirting, no more remarks that are personal."

"Aw, shucks," he drawled, making her chuckle. "Where's the fun in that?"

"Humor me. I caused the last crisis, but we can avoid future ones."

"If my kisses are a 'crisis,' then I have no intentions of avoiding flirting with you."

"Go get the beer and lemonade," she said quietly, wanting to end the volatile conversation that could put them back in each other's arms easily.

She watched him walk away, a masculine stride that was purposeful, hinting of the excellent physical condition he must be in.

Her thoughts were filled with guilt. Why, oh, why had she flirted with him so openly when she had known what the consequences would be?

She couldn't understand her reaction to him, couldn't explain it. It didn't happen with other men, but that definitely did not make Jake "Mr. Right." He was Mr. Wrong in so many ways.

She thought about her grandmother who would be shaking her head and frowning at the idea of spending an evening in the company of a Benton. She never could have explained a relationship with a Benton to her grandmother. Grandmother had been furious with Will for going out with Brittany Benton.

If Will knew she was with Jake tonight, he would be disgusted because of the lifelong competition between the two in school and sports. Then again, perhaps he would shrug it off that she was spending time with Jake because Will also held a low opinion of her, as well. She thought Will had been dazzled by Brittany at first. She also suspected he liked sneaking around, getting away with something that would annoy both families because it stirred talk and envy among his peers.

Jake returned with a cold bottle of beer for himself and a tall, frosty glass of lemonade for her, placing the drinks on a table in front of the sofa.

Only a few feet away, he sat, facing her, and taking a drink of beer.

"The lemonade is delicious."

"I can't take credit. I have a cook."

"Does your cook live in town?"

"Nope. His wife cooks for the men on the ranch and they live in a house here on the ranch. Our foreman also has a house of his own. We've got a big complex with several homes."

"I noticed when I came in."

"I meant it when I said you could have been arrested for trespassing if you had been caught."

"I figured since I obviously wasn't coming to steal livestock and I'm a woman, they would give me time to explain what I was doing and at worst, run me off your property. I really didn't expect to get arrested. Besides, the sheriff is a cousin of my foreman."

Jake smiled. "You're probably right then. It's a long ride by horseback."

"Whatever it takes to talk to the untouchable Benton."

"Definitely never untouchable to you. I'll be happy to convince you just how 'touchable' I am," he teased.

"Don't you dare," she answered, smiling at him. He caught a lock of her hair, twisting it in his fingers and causing slight tugs on her scalp that were as noticeable as every other physical contact.

"So, Caitlin, what do you want in your future?" Jake asked.

"To continue my photography. To marry and have a family."

"What happens to the photography when you marry and have a family?"

"I'll juggle them the way others do. I have leeway to set my own hours for a lot of my work. What's your future, Jake? No marriage, no family, continue to make money."

"Right. No change, really."

"You've grown up in basically the same surroundings I have, yet our families have been totally different. You have a controlling father and siblings. My father didn't want to acknowledge my existence and my grandmother raised me. I have a half brother, but I might as well be an only child, because Will cared nothing for me."

"That must have hurt."

She gazed into blue eyes that hid his feelings. He looked as impassive as if talking about the weather. "I was adopted when I was only weeks old, so I have had my grandmother all my life and she showered love on me. I was happy with her and loved her totally. It hurt to be snubbed and rejected, but not deeply. I don't feel scarred from it. I just don't want it to happen again to a child of mine," she said, facing Jake and getting a strange feeling inside. Seduction could lead to an unexpected pregnancy, a baby born out of wedlock, just as she had been. She didn't want that to happen to a child of hers and the one way to ensure it didn't, was to stay out of any man's bed.

"So seduction is out of the question tonight," Jake remarked lightly as if teasing her, but she was certain the remark was made in earnest.

"Most definitely," she answered quickly. How easily she answered, yet how difficult it was to stick by her resolution.

They sat and talked with Jake touching locks of her hair or her shoulder or lightly caressing her nape. Casual touches that she didn't care to draw attention to, yet they were fanning flames. Finally, she stood. "Jake, it's late. I should turn in."

"Sure, I'll show you a guest bedroom."

When she walked with him down a long hall, he pointed out different rooms. She stopped to look at an enormous dining room with a table that would seat thirty, a cathedral ceiling and a stone fireplace. "Do you ever have this many guests to fill this table?"

"Yes. Parties. There are times I have a lot of company out here. Gabe and I will have things together. There are family parties, too."

"Do your parents spend much time here?"

"Nope. Dad has a ranch in the Hill Country where the area is green and scenic. This place was our family ranch, but Dad deeded it to me and gave Gabe another one he owned."

She nodded. "How nice. A father who passes things on to more than the oldest child. Of course, mine wouldn't have passed anything on to me if I had been the oldest child. I told you, I never dreamed Will would sell the place. Neither did our father who would have put binding stipulations on Will had he known. I'm sure he assumed Will would always live there. He left money to me, but nothing else. No part of the ranch."

"I'll have to admit, I'm glad Will sold out. Our family has wanted that ranch for generations. The sale has brought you into my life, which is a bonus."

They strolled down the wide hall again until he turned into a suite. "These are my rooms. You'll be nearby, but I wanted you to see where I am." She looked at the living area that held a desk, an entertainment center, comfortable sofas and chairs, a wall of bookshelves. On a nearby table she noticed a picture of a beautiful brown-haired woman standing beside a horse.

"That's my sister," he said quietly. "We were close."

Caitlin moved closer to study the picture. "She's beautiful." She understood why Will had gotten involved with her. "She's really gorgeous," she said, thinking she was the feminine version of Jake with blue eyes and brown hair. Caitlin had known about Brittany Benton and Will because sometimes Will had made her cover for him when he had slipped away from family gatherings, and she could remember Brittany as one of the most beautiful girls she had known. Caitlin was aware that Will had been happy and seemingly in love with Brittany at first. She never thought Will concerned himself with the old feud or did anything with Brittany out of revenge. Caitlin was certain that Will did exactly what he wanted to do and family history never mattered to him. Since she had to occasionally be ready to cover for him with the family, she knew when he had been out with Brittany.

Brittany had always been nice to her, and Caitlin had wondered how Will could hold the interest of someone so beautiful and so friendly. Except Will could be charming when he wanted to be. He was with his friends. At first, Will had been wildly happy about dating Brittany. The little Caitlin had seen him, it still was obvious how happy he was. Probably, he had been happy until Brittany had made demands on him. Caitlin could imagine Will carelessly getting Brittany pregnant and then wanting no part of taking any responsibility.

Being with Jake had brought back memories of that time as well as the questions about what had really happened.

Had Will really been driving the car that killed Brittany Benton? If Brittany had been pregnant, Caitlin could see Will becoming desperate to avoid an obligation and the wrath of their father. Deep down, perhaps Grandmother had suspected Will had been responsible, but she always tried to hold the family together. They would never have an answer because the only living person who knew was Will, but Caitlin could imagine him going to any length to live life the way he wanted.

Caitlin's grandmother had always wondered even though she only said it aloud once. They had been talking about the trial late at night and Grandmother had gazed out the window into the dark night. "Will is focused on himself," she had said. "He might be capable of wrecking Brittany Benton's car to get her out of his life." Caitlin had listened in shocked silence. After a few minutes, Grandmother had turned back to look at Caitlin. "This family will stand by Will. He has to be proven innocent."

"I remember at Will's trial, Grandmother had gathered the family. We all had to go to support Will."

"Yeah, our family did the same to show support for Brittany even though she wasn't present," Jake said and his tone was cold.

"My dad always insisted that Will was innocent. We celebrated Will's being found innocent of all charges. That was the one time I recall when Will was nice to me the entire evening. It was one of the few times I can remember seeing him at his best."

"Sorry. I can't agree."

Was Jake trying to get revenge by buying the place and tearing down all the structures, destroying everything owned by the Santerres that he could?

Her grandmother would be shocked, certainly annoyed that Caitlin was here, planning to spend the night with a Benton. Not as annoyed as the men in the family. Will hated Jake and Jake indicated the dislike was mutual. She had heard all about Brittany Benton and Will, whispers from Ginny McCorkin, her best friend, as well as her grandmother's side of the story. Rumors were that Will had gotten Brittany pregnant and refused to marry her. Grandmother had been furious with Will, but she seldom saw Will once he was a teen. Caitlin always figured Brittany was pregnant because of carelessness on Will's part. Will was too selfish to worry about someone else, even when he thought he was in love. Will wanted to stop seeing Brittany, difficult when she lived on the neighboring ranch and didn't want to stop seeing him. Then the fatal night when Will and Brittany had fought when she had died in the car wreck.

Both sides had a battery of lawyers, the Santerres' from Chicago, the Bentons' attorneys from Los Angeles. Will was found innocent and released, all charges dropped, but the hatred between the two families had grown stronger and the animosity between Will and Jake had become worse than ever.

She recalled the trial. Grandmother Santerre had insisted the entire family attend to show support for eighteen-year-old Will. The Bentons had turned out, too, all of them looking solemn and angry. Seventeen-year-old Jake and his brother, his mother and father. Will's mother had still been alive then. She had attended with Titus. Caitlin had been there with Grandmother. They had cousins from Dallas and an aunt and uncle who had come to show support for Will. It had been a solemn time. Caitlin could recall feeling sorry for Brittany and for the mess Will had created. Deep down, Caitlin suspected the Bentons had the true story. Will had a cruel streak and he was a wild driver. Before the fatal accident, when Will had wrecked cars, she had heard her grandmother arguing with her father about covering for Will and buying him new cars without involving the insurance company. It was always difficult for Caitlin to think that Will was any blood relation to Grandmother Santerre who was kind, loving and caring.

That weekend after the trial Will had gone out to celebrate. She'd heard he had had a big fight with Jake Benton. She never heard who won, but assumed Will because she suspected he was meaner and he was a year older and bigger, but she'd heard stories about Jake Benton, too, and wondered if he had held his own with Will.

Caitlin closed her eyes for a moment to clear her thoughts, then glanced around the room again. "You have everything you want here," she said, hoping to change the subject.

"Yes, I do. It's comfortable and I come here to relax and get away from the regular work and office. This is my first love."

"Then why don't you ranch? You don't have to work like crazy."

He shrugged. "Yes, I do. I want to make money. I want total independence from my dad and there are accomplishments in the business world that will help me get what I want to stay totally independent."

"Like making more money, owning more property, building a bigger company and a few other things along the same lines," she said.

"Right. Let me show you where my bedroom is," he said, taking her arm. She stood, resisting him slightly.

"I think I can find your bedroom, should I need to. If the house catches on fire, I'd guess you have an alarm system."

He grinned. "You can't blame me for trying to get you into my bedroom. I'd like to remember you in there in my arms."

"It's not going to happen. Not tonight at any rate," she added.

"Very well, I'll show you to your room next. Wait a minute."

He left and disappeared into an adjoining room to return with folded clothes and a robe on a hanger. "You can have these tonight."

"Thanks. Some of that is still in a package," she said.

"I keep extras. I told you, I have a lot of company here off and on. By the way, I have motion sensors and alarms that I turn on in the evening. Don't go beyond the end of the hall without letting me know."

"I won't."

He led her to another suite near his. "How's this?"

"Lovely," she said, looking at a cheerful suite with white furniture and brightly covered floral patterns in the chairs, splashes of yellow and green in the decor. "Thanks for the shelter from the storm," she said.

He stepped closer and slipped his arm around her waist. "One good-night kiss isn't the end of the world."

"It'll never stop with one," she whispered, standing on tiptoe as she wound her arm around his neck again. His mouth covered hers and she placed her other arm around his waist, holding him while she kissed him in return. The impact was stronger. Temptation grew, but she stopped him. "Jake, I'll see you in the morning."

He gave a hungry look before brushing a kiss on her cheek as he strolled out. She followed him, keeping a wide distance between them.

In the hall he turned. "I'm glad you came and we didn't just have this appointment at the office. It turned out better that I didn't know you wanted to talk to me."

"You didn't have the long ride from my ranch or try for over twenty calls to get through to you."

"Sorry," he said.

"You're not really. You'll continue keeping out unwanted visitors. See you in the morning, Jake. You can call me at seven o'clock. How's that time?"

"Perfect. Good night," he said and was gone, closing the door behind him.

She stood staring at the door. His presence was overwhelming and the day had been a surprise. She had never expected to find Jake Benton a man she would be attracted to. Would he talk reasonably next week or had he already made up his mind and was simply toying with her?

Would she see him again after his decision? She should complete their business and get out of his life. He would get out of hers soon enough.

As she remembered his kiss, her lips tingled. He had stirred a storm in her, something totally unexpected.

She ran her hand over the pile of clothing. The robe was dark blue velvet, soft and warm. She picked up a package wrapped in tissue with a seal and opened it to find new dark blue silk pajamas and slippers. There was a package with a small hairbrush and comb, new toothbrush in plastic, more toiletries in the plastic from a store.

Caitlin showered and dressed in the silk pajamas, relishing the smooth, soft material against her skin. She slipped into the robe, turned the television on low and curled up in bed to watch, but her thoughts drifted to Jake and she neither saw nor heard the program she had turned on.

She still marveled over the chemistry between them. How could it happen with Jake? It wasn't anything either of them wanted or did one thing to cause. Yet it existed, all right, as apparent as a Roman candle shot into the night sky.

She could only think he would entertain an offer from her to buy back part of the Santerre ranch. Caitlin expected him to make a profit, perhaps a huge one, but she didn't care what the purchase cost. She was well fixed financially, having inherited Grandmother Santerre's fortune, plus the money she made from her photography that was growing each year.

Unless he simply priced it out of the market to keep her from buying, she would pay an exorbitant fee if she had to in order to get the land back. It had been a final cruel snub by Will, selling the place without informing her. She didn't expect to have contact with him ever again.

Her thoughts shifted to Jake and the moment he had stepped out of his car and strolled to his porch, climbing the steps until he was on her level, to gaze into her eyes.

He was far more handsome than she had remembered, but she hadn't seen him for years and as a child, he had just been an older boy. Now he was an incredibly sexy, handsome, appealing man. She didn't want this dynamite reaction to a Benton. Even if none of the arguments and fights had anything to do personally with her.

When Jake had faced her on the porch, she had barely been able to get her breath. His blue-eyed gaze had been riveting. His smile was a flash of warm sunshine. But it was his kisses that took her breath and set her spinning. Kisses that burned and melted and made her want him desperately.

She wanted to be in his arms in his bed right now with Jake making love to her. It was insanity, a slippery slide to disaster. Never in her life did she want to take a chance on leading the life her mother had—rejection by the man she loved, an unplanned pregnancy, giving up her baby, humiliation and hurt. If Grandmother Santerre hadn't been there, Caitlin's life could have been frightful. She was thankful every day for the blessings she had.

Later, she tossed and turned and fell asleep still thinking about Jake and his hot kisses, knowing next week he had agreed to talk to her about buying back part of the ranch. Would he sell to her?

Four

The next morning Caitlin dressed in the same blue shirt and jeans she had worn the day before. She braided her hair into one long rope that hung down her back.

She found Jake in the state-of-the-art kitchen with its cherrywood walls, granite countertops and large glassed-in dining area. He was dressed in jeans and a black knit shirt and was talking on his phone. When her gaze slid over him, her heart skipped faster. He was handsome, far too appealing.

Glancing at her, he motioned her to come in, but she left to give him privacy, walking to the nearest room, which was a sunroom. A yellow bougainvillea grew in a massive pot and climbed up one wall to curl across part of the skylight ceiling. Its yellow blooms were bright, matching the yellow upholstered rattan furniture.

"There you are," Jake said, striding into the room, his presence dominating it. "I motioned to you to come on in. That was no private conversation. It was my friend, Nick

Rafford. We have fathers with similar traits of being control freaks. I got some sympathy and words of wisdom from Nick over my dad's latest demands."

"Sorry. I've never had that problem in my life."

"Be thankful. Come have some breakfast. You look as fresh as if you had just driven here from your home."

"Thank you. I don't quite think so. You may need glasses."

He smiled and walked beside her to the kitchen. In a short time they were seated in the dining area with fluffy eggs and hot buttered toast, tall chilled glasses of orange juice and steaming coffee.

"In fact," he said, "I'm here to get away from my dad. This ranch is a haven."

"Then you can understand how I feel about ours," she said. "It's a retreat even though I'm not trying to escape from any particular person. Just people in general. Do you have this often with your father?"

"Too often to suit me."

"Can't you ignore him?"

Jake shot her a look. "He always sees to it there's a threat that makes it impossible to ignore him."

"A threat?" she asked, beginning to wonder if Jake's father had a streak of meanness like her half brother Will. "Is he like Will? Will can be mean to get his way."

"Depends on what you call mean. Cruel and unusual punishment rather than anything physical. In this case, I will be disinherited."

"Good heavens! What does he want you to do?" she said, staring at Jake and momentarily forgetting her breakfast.

"Get married within the year," Jake answered quietly and she laughed. Jake gave her another grim look. "I'm not joking."

"Sorry. You have to get married or be disinherited? Well,

that's simple enough. Marry someone. You'll inherit a fortune and then you can divorce."

"Oh, no. I have to marry this year and I have to remain married for five years or the deal's off and I'm disinherited. My friend, Nick, has the same sort of father and he made the same kind of demand and Nick just happened to fall in love and marry. My dad knows Nick's father and thought that was an excellent plan—so now he's foisted it on me."

She stared at Jake. "I can't imagine a parent interfering that much, particularly with someone who is as together as you are. You're successful, have friends, have a full life. You're an adult. That decision is highly personal and yours to make. You can't just run out and grab up a wife."

"I have no intention of 'running out and grabbing up a wife' or even marrying if I fall in love. I have my own fortune and this time he's gone too far," Jake stated in a quiet voice that held a cold note of steel. His blue eyes had become glacial. "I'll be damned if I'll marry just to suit my dad. If I fell wildly in love tomorrow, I wouldn't marry this year, not for any reason. I'm calling his hand on this one. He can go ahead and disinherit me. At this point, I don't give a damn." He looked at her for a moment. "How did we get on this subject?"

She was still staring at Jake, horrified that his father would make such a demand and astounded by Jake's attitude. "I can't believe what I'm hearing. You'll give up your father's fortune just to do your own thing in your own way? That's incredible. Will would marry in an instant to avoid being disinherited."

"Do not compare me to your half brother," Jake said, making no effort to hide his annoyance.

"Of course not, sorry," she said, barely thinking about what she was saying as she mulled over a man who would turn down a fortune in order to be his own person and not yield to a demanding father's wishes. "I have to say, I'm impressed."

Jake paused as he was pouring more orange juice. He set

down the pitcher to look at her. The coldness in his expression melted away. "That doesn't help, but it makes me feel better to have someone appreciate my stand."

"I hope you don't fall in love this year. On the other hand, if you do, you might change your mind about the inheritance."

He gave her a cocky grin. "Not much danger of either, but I promise you, I will not marry this year or next for that matter."

She continued to stare at him, unable to fathom his giving up a huge fortune so easily. His father was on lists as one of the wealthiest men in Texas.

"You're staring," he said with amusement. "I'll admit, if it's this startling, you are making me feel better about my decision."

"It is absolutely incredible. I'm trying to think what I would do in the same circumstances. I'm not sure I'd have the willpower to turn down a fortune. It's also depressing because you will not be swayed by money to sell back part of the ranch."

"No. At this point in my life, I'm not easily swayed by money. There are other things in life that entice me," he said and his tone changed and the words took another meaning. Now when she looked into his blue eyes, she saw desire.

"So maybe it's not money I should fling at you for the ranch, but something else, something more personal," she replied in a breathless voice. She was flirting when she knew better. *Leave Jake Benton alone,* she'd ordered herself, yet she couldn't resist the retort and it had an effect as his chest expanded.

"Try me and see what it gets you," he said.

"Maybe I'll do that, Jake." She sipped her juice and lowered the glass. "I think we should get back on a less personal, less flirty basis. I wish I could view life that way. Even though I had a very comfortable life growing up and have

Grandmother's fortune now, I can't be as relaxed about money as you are."

"You have a normal attitude. Besides, when the dust settles, I expect my father to change his mind. But if he doesn't, I'll stick by what I've said."

"I think, Jake Benton, you are an unusual man."

He reached out to tilt her face up to his. "And you, Caitlin, are a beautiful woman. Go to dinner with me tonight. We can fly to Dallas."

"Won't that take a lot of time?" she asked while her heart raced. Dinner with Jake. Foolish, yet it might help win her the ranch.

"I have a plane here. We'll be there in no time. I'll pick you up at a quarter to six."

"A Benton asking out a Santerre. You wouldn't have done that twenty-four hours ago."

"Life changes. I can adapt. So can you."

"Who's the woman in your life right now and what is she doing while you're at the ranch? Will your taking me to dinner interfere in your relationship with her?"

"There is no woman in my life right now. Not one here or in Dallas. I'd think that detective you hired would have told you that item."

"Actually, he did. I just wanted you to confirm it because he could have missed something. That makes me feel better about going out with you."

"I'll look forward to it." His hand slipped behind her head and he moved closer to brush her lips with a light kiss. "Good morning, by the way."

"Good morn—" His mouth covered hers and ended her sentence. Her heart slammed against her ribs. His kiss was slow, hot, igniting desire instantly. While her heart drummed, she relished kissing him. Negatives with Jake ceased to exist.

The only awareness was Jake and sensations he caused. With an effort to grasp safety, she finally ended the kiss.

"How did we get on this footing so swiftly?" she asked, catching her breath. "This time yesterday, I didn't even know you except on sight. And you didn't know me when you saw me. Now we're kissing."

"It happens. Sometimes even faster. The chemistry is there. You feel it, too." He moved away to get the coffeepot and returned to refill their cups. When he sat down, he sipped his juice. "I'll take you home this morning. I've already called the stable to get your horse ready and we'll put him in a trailer."

"Great. I'll be happy to avoid the long ride home. While you're at the house, I want you to meet Cecilia, Kirby and Altheda. I'll call and let them know you're coming."

"That isn't necessary," he said.

"I know. I really want you to meet them."

She ate her breakfast, but her appetite had diminished. The more she was with him, the less likely she thought he would part with his newly acquired property, yet the thought of Jake coming in and tearing down the beloved house turned her to ice. She wasn't going to dwell on that until he gave her an answer about a sale.

"Stop worrying, Caitlin," he said lightly.

"Does it show that much?" she asked, thinking it was sinful for a man to have such thick lashes and such blue eyes.

"Yes, and at this point, it's unnecessary. I haven't made a decision and I want to talk to my brother, Gabe, and our geologist."

"After breakfast, I'll call Altheda to let her know we're coming. I told you about Altheda last night. She's the resident housekeeper and cook. And you'll meet Cecilia, too. She was Grandmother's companion and secretary and long before that, a nanny for me. She's almost part of the family and feels like an great-aunt. I really might as well have been a only child. I can hardly count Will as a sibling even though, legally, he is."

"I don't blame you. I wouldn't count Will as a sibling either, but then I have strong feelings about Will, just as he does about me. I'm still astonished he sold to me."

"I'm sure all Will was thinking about was the money he would get. He wouldn't have cared whose money it was."

"Actually, I think he thought he was getting the best of me by getting my money while I got the ranch. Besides, I was the highest bidder—by far."

"I'm sure he'd view the sale that way. The money was the best of the deal to him."

Jake reached for his coffee. "So does the photography go on hold when you're at the ranch?"

"At the moment, I'm between jobs and I had cleared my schedule, so this is fine. I have to get back to the city soon. I only intended to be here a few days, mainly to see you and discuss the sale."

"I had to get away from Dallas, as well as make myself unavailable to my dad. Now I'm especially glad I did. I just made this decision at the last minute. Your private detective must be a good one. He also must have access to my office or someone very close to me."

"It's not difficult to learn your whereabouts. You don't hide what you do. You flew in your plane and your pilot had a flight plan filed."

Jake nodded. "Interesting. No, I've never had to hide from anyone, so I'm not overly cautious. I keep a relatively low profile anyway."

She laughed. "Right. How many times have I seen your picture on society pages with beautiful women on your arm?"

"Those hardly count."

"The pictures or the women?" Before he could answer, she

said, "I'm teasing you. I know you meant the pictures." She
went on. "I know a few things about you from the detective.
You have close friends you play golf and basketball with.
Let's see if I can remember, Tony Ryder is one close friend.
You mentioned your friend Nick Rafford. Those are the ones
I recall."

"They're my best friends. Plus my brother. I have a bet with
those guys, not my brother, but the others. When we were all
bachelors we agreed to each bet a million that we would not
marry. The last to marry wins the pot."

She laughed. "So if you marry, you lose a million dollars
in a bet and if you don't marry you lose millions in your
inheritance. You'll lose either way, Jake. How did you get
yourself into that?"

He grinned. "I think the million is the smallest loss. Also
the least likely."

"And your friend Nick is married?"

"Married a woman who was guardian of his baby nephew
and she and Nick had a baby. Now he's married and the father
of two."

"May you have such great fortune," she teased and Jake
rolled his eyes.

"Actually, Nick's really happy. It's been good for him. His
dad is ecstatic, which is why my dad is so eager. Tony's dad is
just as bad. I'm a buffer for Gabe. Dad always focuses on me
while Gabe squeaks by without as much interference. Heaven
help him if I marry and get out of Dad's sights. Enough about
that."

"I can't imagine such a thing. Grandmother let me make
so many of my choices with little direction from her."

"Be thankful." He finished his coffee. "Did you sleep
well?"

"Yes, great," she said, having no intention of telling him
she couldn't get him out of her thoughts; or how she had

wanted his kisses. She wouldn't admit when she had fallen asleep, she had dreamed about him. "And you?"

"Great, but I wasn't in a strange bed in a strange house. This is home to me. Only one thing would have been an improvement," he added with a huskier note entering his voice.

"I'm not asking about that improvement. You had an undisturbed night's sleep. End of subject."

"We're through breakfast. Fred will clean this, so let's get ready to go."

"I can't shake the feeling you're putting me off about discussing a purchase," she said, knowing she should drop it until he wanted to talk. She couldn't get it out of mind more than a few minutes at a time.

"I've told you that we'll talk, but I want to think about it first."

"It seems incredibly simple to me. Sell me a small chunk of the ranch. Deal done. You'll never miss it."

"Maybe."

"Surely you don't want me out of this area. I have never done anything to hurt you," she said, carrying her dishes to the sink in spite of what he'd said.

He caught her wrist as she set down the dishes and reached for the faucet. "I told you, no cleaning. And no, you've never done one thing to hurt me, nor has your grandmother. It's your father and Will that I have strong feelings about."

"Oh, surely, you can't mean that you would hold that land just because I have the same name as Will." She looked into unfathomable blue eyes and wondered how strong his hatred was.

"No, I don't, Caitlin," he said quietly and something inside her unclenched.

"I'm glad," she said, realizing in first one way and then another, he was gaining her liking and her respect. He already stirred desire. It was becoming a potent and frightening combination because she didn't want to care about Jake Benton or have her heart race when he looked at her. Scariest of all was admiring and liking him.

"With oil hanging in the balance, I just want to give some thought to my decision."

"We both have old demons to get past," she said.

"I agree. We've spent a lifetime hating each other's families. It's difficult to switch that off instantly. You rode over here angry with me all the way, didn't you?"

"Yes, as a matter of fact, I did. I've told you why—all those messages I left for you ignored by your employees."

"I'll have to talk to someone about that. Maybe they need to find out a little more about the person before they turn them away. On the other hand, I don't think anyone would have reported to me that a very gorgeous woman was being told she couldn't even have a phone conversation with me."

"Don't be ridiculous." Caitlin smiled.

He turned her to face him. "I'm not being ridiculous. You wouldn't have stood a chance at getting me to sell any land back to you if we hadn't met in person, I can truthfully tell you that. I've always lumped you in with your father and half brother."

"Big mistake," she said. "But then Grandmother didn't like your family, so there you are. I didn't, either."

"Hopefully, that has changed forever for you."

"Time will tell," she said.

"That's a reserved answer, Caitlin," he said, studying her.

"My guess is, you feel the same way. You can't expect me to be overjoyed with you if you turn me down and I'm definitely not saying that as an ultimatum."

"Let's not get into conflict when it isn't necessary," he said

His cell phone buzzed and he answered to talk briefly before placing it in his pocket again.

"The car, trailer and horse are waiting. Shall we go?" he asked. As they left the house, they emerged into a clear day with water still dripping from trees and the rooftops.

They reached the truck and Jake held her door while she climbed inside. In a short time they were on the highway and she thought of the long ride to his ranch on horseback and how angry and determined she had been to see him.

As they sped toward her ranch, she studied his profile. His stand toward his father's unreasonable demand, his care for his sister and brother—she envied that slightly because she had never had any love or even much kindness or attention from Will. Those things softened her harsh feelings toward the Bentons. Plus the wild unwanted allurement that had captured both of them.

Jake was turning out to be so different from the man she had imagined him to be. Much more appealing. Yet beneath all the good things lay their past history. He was a Benton who had done unacceptable things to Santerres. Will's dislike of Jake and competition with him in sports and school was legendary. Maybe both had excelled simply because they were each trying to outdo the other.

Soon they were on what had once been Santerre land, and she grew more tense with each mile. She wanted to keep her house, keep the people who had worked for her grandmother. Damn Will and his selfish ways and the ultimate cruelty in selling all this to Jake without giving her any chance to buy part of it.

"In a way, I'm surprised Will would sell you the mineral rights."

"I wouldn't have bought the ranch otherwise, but Will told me there's no oil. His father had geologists study the land, even leased it at one point, but they gave up and said there was no oil."

"What about natural gas?"

Jake smiled at her. "As far as Will's concerned, if there's no oil, there's no gas. Will is into buildings and cities and finance, not oil, gas and wind. Or even water rights. There's a lot of water on your ranch."

"I can't believe Will's lawyers let him do this without giving him a lot of advice that was solid."

"Your brother doesn't strike me as the type to take advice well. Not even from men he hires to give it to him."

She nodded. "You're right. Will is supremely confident. It helps him in many ways, but sometimes it blinds him."

"You're so much younger. I'm surprised you were around him often."

"I wasn't, but we had family gatherings because my father was the darling of my grandmother."

"What about you?"

"Oh, yes. She was wonderful to me. I'm a granddaughter, the daughter she never had. But she loved my father with all her being. He loved her, too, so we were together on holidays where Will made his presence felt. I hated being with him because when I was little, he was mean. He'd pinch me or thump me. When I'd cry, he'd deny he had done anything. He'd say I was pretending until Grandmother lectured him. With someone checking on him, he left me alone, but he was never nice, never a brother. Since she passed, he's barely spoken to me."

"Will is something else," Jake said with disgust in his voice.

When they topped a hill, a tall three-story Victorian house came into view. Trees surrounded it and shaded the steeply sloped rooftops, gables, balconies and wide bay windows.

"See, Jake, it's a beautiful old house built by the first Santerre."

"That wasn't the first house," he said.

"There's a tiny log house that was the first, but in time, this house was built. The family considers it the first real ranch house."

She wanted Jake to see the house, meet the people who worked for her and had devoted years to her grandmother. It should be much more difficult for Jake to displace them if he knew them, rather than faceless, nameless entities.

They drove to the corral where a wiry, sandy-haired man with streaks and sideburns of gray came forward to greet her. His weathered face was tan from years in the sun.

"Jake, meet our foreman, Kirby Lenox," she said when she stepped out of the truck and greeted Kirby. "Kirby, this is Jake Benton."

She watched the two shake hands and Kirby size up Jake. She saw no reaction from Jake except a friendly greeting, but she suspected he was taking in everything he saw to help him make his decision about her place.

"I'll get the horse now. It won't take long and then you two can go on to the house," Kirby told them.

As he backed the horse out of the trailer, Jake watched. "That's a fine horse," he said, looking over her bay.

"This one's a dandy. Caitlin has a keen eye for a horse."

"That's because I learned from you," she said, smiling at Kirby.

He grinned as he patted the horse. "He's a fine one. He's Caitlin's favorite. Nice to meet you, Mr. Benton."

"It's Jake, Kirby. We'll see each other again," he said easily as he held the pickup door for Caitlin.

She felt as if she were walking on broken glass, treading carefully, hoping Jake would appreciate the old house and the people or at least like them even half as much as she did.

"Thanks," she said. In minutes Jake stopped in front of the house and walked around to open her door. He took her arm in a light touch that was a blistering contact.

"Come look around," she said, gazing with satisfaction at the porch with wooden rockers, swings, pots of blooming flowers. Lacy gingerbread spindles formed the posts and lacy curtains were pulled back inside the bay windows. Caitlin sighed, wondering how anyone could resist the house's charm.

"This is too beautiful to bulldoze," she said as they crossed the porch. "I don't think a Benton has ever been in this house," she added, knowing this was another twist in the history of the family feud.

When he didn't answer, she became silent. The door swung open and Caitlin faced Cecilia whose big brown eyes went from her to Jake and back to Caitlin. "I'm back. Cecilia, I want you to meet Jake Benton."

"Mr. Benton, welcome to Caitlin's home," Cecilia said warmly, extending her hand to Jake who smiled as he took her hand.

"Jake, this is Cecilia Mayes. I've told you about her," Caitlin said, studying the two of them. Jake sounded incredibly polite, not the least a hard-hearted owner who would evict them. He towered over Cecilia who was only five feet tall, small-boned and thin. She wore a flowered cotton housedress and sandals. Her gray hair was fastened behind her head in a bun. She looked as sweet as she actually was to everyone and Caitlin loved her deeply and wanted to protect her from harm.

"I'm glad to meet you, ma'am," Jake said politely. "Please just call me Jake."

"Certainly," she said. "Come in, please. We can sit in the front parlor and I hope you'll stay for lunch with us. I told Altheda to plan for that."

"Thank you, but I should get home before then. I can sit a minute and visit."

"Fine," she said.

"Cecilia, I want to take Jake to meet Altheda and show him a little of the house. Then we'll join you in the front parlor."

"Of course," Cecilia said.

"I want you to see some of the inside of this house," she told Jake when she was alone with him. "The original house is over a hundred years old. Grandmother made changes, had closets built in, added a wing, a deck and pool, an entertainment center. I've added an office. Even so, a lot is still the same."

Fresh flowers from the garden were on the dining room table, visible from the wide hall when they walked through the open door. Jake's Western boots scraped the polished plank floor. Tempting smells of baking bread wafted in the air and Caitlin was pleased by the appearance of the house.

Deep red velvet chairs circled the mahogany dining table. Cut glass and silver filled a breakfront.

"This room was off limits to me as a very small child unless I was invited to eat in here with the family. We had holiday gatherings fairly often when I was small. There won't be any now or anytime in the future."

"I remember our family get-togethers, tedious to mind my manners, yet fun in teasing Brittany and Gabe when they couldn't get back at me."

"Will did that anytime he was here. The first few times I told on him, he denied everything and I got in trouble, so I just learned to endure his mischief. Only he was mean, pinching me during the family prayer when he knew I wouldn't yell, mean tricks he could get away with."

"The bastard," Jake said.

"That's what Will called me far too often when no one else could hear him. If he got a chance, he reminded me that

I was born out of wedlock and neither of my parents wanted me enough to keep me."

She hoped she kept emotion out of her voice, but it was difficult even after all these years to be unemotional about Will's accusations that actually were on target.

"Thank heavens for my grandmother," Caitlin added.

"She gave you almost as much as your father could have given you. If he had taken you in, you would have had to live under the same roof as Will and you would never have known your grandmother as well as you did."

"I've thought of that many times. Were I given a choice to live my life over with Dad or again with Grandmother, I would pick my life with Grandmother. It was a happy time growing up and she was loving and wonderful to me."

"She didn't have the same charitable attitude toward my father."

"Definitely not. She disliked him enormously because of the beating he gave my dad."

"Our families have a long and violent history," Jake remarked.

"I don't know if either of us can ever view the other without thinking about our bloodlines," she said.

"I definitely can look at you and forget," Jake said softly. "When I am near you, that old feud is the last thing I'm thinking about."

"I'm not pursuing what you are thinking about," she stated with a laugh. "Let me show you more of the house.

"Here's the kitchen," she said, entering a room she loved with a high ceiling and glass-fronted cabinets. Floor-to-ceiling glass gave a panoramic view of the pool and a decorator-designed deck.

Two ceiling fans slowly revolved. A woman in a black uniform with a white apron turned to smile at them. In her hand she held a tray from the oven with tempting-looking brownies.

"Jake, this is Altheda Perkins who has worked here since she was seventeen. Altheda, meet Jake Benton, the man who now owns the ranch."

"Glad to meet you Mr. Benton," she said politely, her smile fading slightly for a brief moment and then returning. Her white hair was a mass of curls framing her face. "Would either of you care for a brownie and milk? I can bring them to the front parlor."

Jake declined at the same time Caitlin did. "We both just finished breakfast. Perhaps later this morning, we might enjoy a bite."

To Jake she said, "The cabinets in here are the originals. The glass fronts are more trouble to take care of, but Altheda is willing and I love them."

"Nice kitchen," he said, looking around. The appliances were as up-to-date as his own, yet the kitchen retained the charm and appearance of another century and Caitlin loved every inch of it.

Caitlin showed him the new part of the house only briefly, dwelling more on the original and older rooms and areas. She tried to make him see that he would be destroying a treasure if he tore it down.

Beyond a polite interest, she couldn't detect any other feelings about what he was seeing. She loved her grandmother's house more than any other place and couldn't see it as anything except a precious home that should be maintained and enjoyed.

How steeped was Jake in the hatred that always lay smoldering between the two families?

She led him through downstairs rooms and then they returned to join Cecilia in the parlor.

Jake sat, talking politely to Cecilia, laughing at a story

she told that had involved him in town. Occasionally as they talked, Caitlin glanced at her watch or the clock on the mantel and was gratified to see that an hour had passed and Jake not only showed no signs of leaving, but seemed to be enjoying himself talking to Cecilia.

Altheda appeared with brownies, a pot of steaming coffee, mugs and saucers.

Jake made a phone call and let Caitlin talk him into staying for lunch.

It was after two in the afternoon when he said he had to get back to the ranch and Caitlin went out to his truck with him.

He held her arm to walk around to his side. "I'd like to walk off into the woods with you or the nearest shed or anywhere we could be alone."

"I don't need to ask why in the world you'd want to do that," she replied, amused, wanting the same thing herself, which she would never admit to him. "I don't think that's possible. You'll be alone with me tonight."

"I'll be at a restaurant with people everywhere."

"I think you'll manage. I'm glad you stayed today and visited with Cecilia."

"She's sweet and reminds me of my grandmother on my mother's side. She knows a lot about people in these parts."

"Cecilia used to get out a lot, go to town and she had many friends. She's become more reclusive in the last years."

He ran his hand across Caitlin's shoulder. "I'll see you in a few hours. Thanks again for lunch."

"Thanks for taking me in during the storm and hearing my plea finally."

He nodded and climbed into his truck and drove away. She walked to the porch and stood watching the truck on the road to the highway.

Cecilia came out to stand beside her. "Caitlin, watch out. He'll break your heart if you're not careful."

Startled, Caitlin turned. "I won't let that happen. I barely know him."

"He's a charming man. He's also accustomed to getting what he wants. Not one word was mentioned about selling land back to you, so I assume he's put you off with an answer."

"Yes, he has until this week when he can talk to his brother and some people at his office."

"He's dangling you along. He wants you and this ranch. I don't think he's going to sell to you."

"Whatever happens," Caitlin said, growing somber over hearing her own sentiments spoken aloud by Cecilia, "I promise, I'll take care of you and Altheda. Kirby, too."

"We can all manage. Your grandmother left us each a trust that will take care of us financially. We'll get along." Cecilia's gaze ran over the porch and tears filled her eyes. "I love this old house and I know you do, too," she said gently. "It may just be time for all of us to let go and move on. Change is life, Caitlin. You know that. You've done your best to win him over, but those Bentons are a hard-hearted bunch toward the Santerres. He hates your brother. It shows in his cold blue eyes."

"Cecilia, Jake isn't so awfully cold," Caitlin said, having a strange feeling of not being truthful. She had a knot in her throat and hated to hear what she feared voiced aloud.

"Just don't fall in love with him, honey. You're going out with him tonight. You be careful. That man doesn't have your interests at heart. At least not now."

"It's just dinner and I'll be careful," Caitlin promised, looking into Cecilia's worried brown eyes. They both stepped closer to hug each other and Caitlin could feel Cecilia's thin shoulders and hurt for her. "Cecilia, I'd do anything to keep him from uprooting you and the others," she said, fighting tears.

"Don't," Cecilia said firmly, pulling away and holding Caitlin's shoulders. "Do not do anything foolish to get your way. He'll take advantage of you and hurt you. We'll all be fine and stop worrying about us. You've talked to him about selling and you've done your part."

Caitlin nodded. "I better check my calls and emails. I haven't since this morning."

"You'll have to put it off for a few more minutes because here comes Kirby," Cecilia said. "I'm going in. He'll want to talk to you, not me. I'm guessing he's in his fatherly mode. We all want to keep you from getting hurt while you're trying to protect us."

Caitlin saw the foreman striding toward her, a lanky, relaxed walk that still covered ground rapidly. She had a sinking feeling he might want to air his feelings and warn her to be careful around Jake, too.

Cecilia left and in minutes Kirby climbed the porch steps to lean against a post facing her as she sat and gently rocked.

"I saw Benton drive away. I hear he's taking you out tonight."

Caitlin couldn't keep from smiling. "You three have a grapevine that carries news faster than text messaging."

He shrugged one shoulder. "Altheda told me. She had lunch for the boys and me and I was up here to get it and talked to her."

"And she must have just found out from Jake's remarks. Yes, I'm going out with him and I'll be fine."

"Look, you're doing this for the three of us, primarily. Dusty and Red, too, because the outcome will impact them. Jake Benton's a tough man. I've ridden against him in rodeos. I've seen Will come up against him and end up the worse for it. I'd say you forget trying to save this place. I don't want to see you hurt."

"Kirby, you're like an older brother to me—or a dad."

"I believe at my age, dad is a better comparison," he said and she smiled fleetingly, her mind on his warning.

"I'll take care of myself and I don't want any of you to worry. Jake won't hurt me. I'm not getting that involved with him."

"He's broken more than a few hearts in this county," Kirby said.

She gazed to the east, thinking about Jake driving home to his ranch.

"I'll be careful. You stop worrying. I've already been warned by Cecilia."

"You might as well give up on him selling the place. That man isn't going to let you have it back. Trucks are pouring in here at that rig where they are drilling. I've watched them with binoculars from the barn loft. They're busy as can be. I wouldn't be surprised if they do find oil. Your dad never thought there was any here, but that time they drilled it was far over in the eastern corner, not up here near the house. They find oil, you can forget any hope of getting part of this ranch back."

"I know. He retains all mineral rights, so he could go right ahead."

"It's not conducive to raising cattle."

"I couldn't just give up without asking. Just please, don't you worry."

Kirby straightened up. "All right. I've said my say and I'll head back to work." He turned and went down the porch steps.

"Kirby—" She waited until he turned around to meet her gaze. "Thank you. I love you for watching out for me."

"You take care, Caitlin. I can't watch out enough to protect you."

She nodded and he walked away, heading back to the barn. Shortly he was in the truck and drove off on one of the ranch's paths.

With a sigh, she went inside, mulling over the warnings against Jake that reaffirmed her own reactions. Neither Kirby nor Cecilia expected Jake to sell back to her. She headed to the kitchen, knowing she might as well listen now to Altheda, hear her cautions and then she could go back to her work to check on her galleries and orders.

When she finally stepped inside her office, she closed the door. Feeling drained, she was more worried than ever about the future of the ranch.

Caitlin soon gave up trying to work because she couldn't keep her mind on anything except Jake. Memories of his kisses tormented her. Questions about his decision concerning the ranch were as constant a concern. All the time she bathed and dressed, she moved as if only half conscious of her actions. Kirby's and Cecilia's warnings made her view the evening with more caution, big reminders to be careful.

In spite of the warnings, her pulse speeded at the prospect. Her feelings toward Jake were mixed; fear he would destroy the place she loved, attraction, family hatreds, excitement. The dinner date would give her another chance to try to talk him into selling. What was really holding him back? Was he trying to get something from her besides a payment? Seduction? Perhaps tonight would bring answers.

Five

With his thoughts on Caitlin, Jake turned into his ranch road and answered a call on his cell. He talked briefly to his brother Gabe who had flown in and was waiting to see him.

When Jake parked, Gabe came out on the porch. His dark brown hair was windblown. He was dressed casually in jeans, boots and a cotton shirt. His blue eyes held curiosity when Jake climbed the porch steps.

"I brought the geological papers, the maps, the description of the barns and outbuildings used by Madeline Santerre. What gives that you're having second thoughts about it?"

"I met Caitlin Santerre and she's asked me to sell part of the property back to her. I'm dragging my feet to see if you find oil."

"Why would you want to consider selling, oil or no oil? We've talked about the possibilities of oil on that land and we've already started drilling."

"We'd retain all mineral, wind and water rights."

"And she would agree to that and still want to buy back part of it?"

"Yep. She wants it for sentimental reasons and to take care of the elderly crew who have worked there."

"Sentimental reasons? You believe that? A sentimental Santerre?"

"This isn't Will. I've found a Santerre who is not like Will at all. I always heard the Grandmother wasn't like her son or grandson. Let's go to the study where we can be comfortable."

"Sure," Gabe said, holding the door and following Jake inside.

"Actually, Will sold it without telling her. They've never gotten along."

"Caitlin Santerre is Titus Santerre's daughter. I've always heard her mother was a Santerre maid."

"That's right. When the maid had the baby Titus didn't want any part of either mother or baby and paid the maid to go away. When she planned to put the baby up for adoption, the grandmother, Madeline Santerre, Titus's mother, adopted her. Thus Caitlin became a Santerre and was raised by Grandmother Santerre. She's told me that Will was never kind to her."

"That can't surprise you."

"Nope. Will is mean through and through. Caitlin is not one bit like Will. She's worrying about the people who worked for Madeline. As far as I can tell, she doesn't have any meanness or selfishness in her."

"Caitlin Santerre. All I remember is a little kid," Gabe said as they entered the study and Jake sat in a leather chair.

"Not so little. I'm taking her to dinner tonight."

"Caitlin? How old is she? I think of her as twelve at the most."

"When you were having birthdays, Caitlin was having birthdays. She's twenty-eight."

"Damn. Twenty-eight? I don't remember seeing her around these parts since she was little." Gabe hooked one knee over the arm of the chair and let his booted foot dangle while he studied Jake. "Why are you taking her to dinner? Why didn't you just tell her no and be on your way?"

"She's beautiful. I want the evening with her."

Gabe's eyebrows arched. "You've hated the Santerres, particularly since Brittany's death. What's the deal here—a little revenge by seducing a Santerre?"

"No. Will doesn't care a thing about her. No revenge there. I just want the evening with her."

Gabe's eyes narrowed as he stared at his brother. "That one I can't figure. You know plenty of beautiful women. You hate the Santerres with a passion. Is there anything you're not telling me?"

"Not a thing. If you could see her, you'd know why I want to go out with her."

Gabe shook his head. "You're not convincing me. I've seen you fight with Will. I've seen you try to beat him in sports. I've heard you call him names and complain about him. You don't like any of them. There's something else."

"Nope."

Gabe became silent and Jake waited patiently for his answers to soak in with his brother.

"Tell her no you won't sell and get on with your life," Gabe said finally. "You're not going to go out often with the woman or have a relationship with her."

"I'll tell her no soon. Probably this week at the office, but tonight, I'm taking her out. If it goes well tonight, I might put her off for a week and go out with her next weekend."

"I can't believe I'm hearing this," Gabe said. "You're sure she isn't going to talk you into selling back to her?"

"Fairly positive."

"Then why the maps and descriptions and pictures?"

"If you must know, she's gaining some of my sympathy. I started out avoiding a definite rejection because I wanted to go out with her. She's gorgeous."

"So you said," Gabe remarked dryly.

"Now, I'm listening to her. If you don't find oil, it doesn't seem such a big deal to sell a patch of land and the old house to her if we retain rights. If you find oil, that house and everyone living in it will be in the way."

"The more you get to know her, the more likely you are to do what she wants."

"Maybe. Maybe not. I don't intend to sell if you find oil."

"That's good because that house of hers may be in the middle of a very lucrative field. I think it is. Before too many more days, we'll know if I'm right."

"I hope you are," Jake said.

"If I am, you won't want her owning any part of the ranch. We'll want to drill where we can get oil. We have to have trucks able to get in and out. I'm puzzled, but okay. I know you're not going all soft over a Santerre. No way is that happening."

"I'm just thinking about it and waiting to hear something decisive from you," Jake said and Gabe smiled.

"I hope I have news for you soon," Gabe remarked. He stood. "I've got to run. I'm flying back to Fort Worth to meet some guys for dinner."

Jake walked to the porch with Gabe. "See you in Dallas."

When his brother was gone, Jake returned to the study to look at the papers Gabe had delivered to him. He hated Will with a passion, disliked Will's father. Why bother selling to Caitlin? He wasn't ready to get her out of his life yet. Erotic images of Caitlin in his bed set his heart drumming.

He had asked to see the house and property because he was

stalling to hear from Gabe about oil before he was forced to give her an answer, yet she had wanted to show him the house and everything else, playing on his sympathy.

She had tried to familiarize him with the house and property so it would not seem impersonal and easy to dispose of. He had allowed her to because the more he was with her, the more he wanted to be with her and to seduce her.

As she had led the way from room to room, he had watched the gentle sway of her hips. He wanted her in his arms in his bed. His blood heated at the thought of tonight. Seduce her, spend time with her and then tell her no.

Would she trade sleeping with him for an agreement from him to sell the house back to her? Or become his mistress for a limited time? The possibility was erotic, tempting. She wanted the house and part of the property in the worst way. It was leverage to get something in return from her and money meant nothing. If it had been Will who wanted the property back, he would have delighted in saying no, but it wasn't Will. This was an entirely different matter. It hinged on Gabe finding oil.

Caitlin had not won him over beyond it being exciting to be with her.

It was a small matter to sell a little piece of the ranch back to her, but he wasn't ready to do so yet. He was certain when he did, he would see no more of Caitlin.

What kind of evening would he have with her? He glanced at his watch. Only a few hours and he would find out.

Caitlin studied herself in the mirror while her thoughts remained only half on her appearance. The prospect of an evening with Jake both excited and disturbed her. Reactions poles apart like all of her responses since she had first faced him. She wanted to get her property back and be done with him because he was an unwanted temptation in her life.

Focusing on her reflection, she smoothed the deep blue long-sleeved dress over her hips. The dress had a draped neckline with a low-cut back. She stepped into silver high-heeled sandals. Her hair was piled on her head, held with a silver clip with a few strands escaping to frame her face. Blue-and-silver earrings dangled from her ears.

A flight to Dallas to eat and then back, but it would be no surprise if he wanted her to stay the night in Dallas. At the thought, her already bubbling insides gave another jump.

The front door knocker made a clang that she could hear upstairs in her bedroom. Grabbing up her clutch purse, she hurried downstairs. Cecilia had already greeted Jake and was in the front room talking to him.

Caitlin heard their voices before she entered the room. Jake stood the minute she walked through the door. Her breathing altered as she looked at Jake in a charcoal suit with a red tie. Even when she was in high heels, he was still the taller. Wickedly handsome, he presented an enormous challenge: win him over about selling—resist seduction.

Then she saw the perusal he was giving her with approval definitely in his warm gaze. "You're beautiful, Caitlin. I can't believe you're the same little kid I remember."

"Thank you. The same little kid you ignored, is what you mean."

"Cecilia, it was nice to see you again, if only briefly."

"Take care tonight," Cecilia said, following them to the door and telling them goodbye. The minute the door closed behind them, Jake took her arm.

"Cecilia looks sweet, but I wouldn't want to meet her in a dark alley. I think she would gladly do me in."

Caitlin laughed. "I have never heard such a description of her in my life. Next to my grandmother, she's the sweetest person on earth."

"You can't tell me I got approval after my visit this

afternoon. That was a frosty few minutes before you arrived."

"Cecilia? I can't believe it. She is always sweet to people. Even Will—she never trusted Will, but she was always kind about him because she knew Grandmother loved him."

"I'm not going to pin you down on Cecilia's opinion of me, but I'd bet the ranch I'm on target."

"You might be," she said, amused by his reaction to Cecilia. "Now if you sell the land back to us, she'll change her opinion completely."

"Ah, that's what her coldness is about. I was afraid it was about taking you out."

"Why would she worry about that?" Caitlin asked.

Jake shot her a look before returning his attention to the ranch road. "Don't make me sound like someone so run-of-the-mill."

She laughed. "You will never be 'run-of-the-mill.' Stop fishing for reassurance or compliments. If our relatives could see us now, they wouldn't believe their eyes. A Benton and a Santerre together for an evening."

"All I can see is a man and a gorgeous woman. That feud melted away when you appeared on my porch."

She smiled as she watched him drive. She had caught a whiff of his woodsy aftershave. All she could remember when she was a kid was an unfriendly older boy who was a Benton and someone to avoid. Not the breathtaking dream sitting only feet away from her and spending the evening with her.

"A penny for your thoughts," he said.

"No amount of money would wring my thoughts out of me right now," she replied, smiling and received another swift glance.

"Now I have to know. Your thoughts must be personal, must involve me and must include tonight."

"You're enough on target that I think we will change the subject. Do you work all the time in Dallas?"

"A large part, but I travel, too. And you're not getting off the hook that easily. Thoughts that concern us and you won't tell me. That's intriguing. Something you don't want to admit."

"Stop it, Jake," she said with a laugh.

"Not when a beautiful woman admits to thoughts about us that she can't confess. That conjures up all sorts of images—"

"You can stop now. You win—I was merely thinking how handsome you are and that we're headed for an exciting evening. There—very ordinary thoughts that could be expected."

"You're not fooling me. You don't want to admit what you're really thinking—more along the lines of speculation about what it would be like to make passionate love," he said, his voice lowering a notch.

She tingled all over. "You won't believe me if I deny that and of course, now you have me thinking about it."

His hand tightened on the steering wheel. Otherwise, she saw no visible sign of reaction to what she'd just said. "Now I wish I had started this conversation when I wasn't driving."

"You brought this on yourself. Perhaps you should take my suggestion and we change the subject."

"Flirting is infinitely more fun with you than an ordinary conversation," he said.

"More dangerous, Jake. You and I were never destined for any kind of future together. We can ignore the feud for a time, but never completely, and it means some things will never take place between us."

"Not necessarily. A kiss can diminish family histories like lightning striking a tree. I'll show you when we return to this conversation when I'm no longer driving."

His words wrapped around her, making her warm. He wouldn't forget what he just said. Kisses awaited, heightening her bubbling excitement.

"I hope you've thought about Grandmother's house. It is so wonderful, Jake. It's filled with memories. I just can't bear to lose it."

"It is a fine old home, Caitlin. There's no argument about that."

They reached his ranch and drove to park in front of an open hangar. Nearby a dazzling white jet waited, a larger craft than she had expected. The moment she stepped inside, she saw it was a luxury jet that held plush seats, tables, a bar, a screen for films, electronic equipment and phones. "This is an elegant plane, Jake."

"It's comfortable and equipped for me to work while I fly. Or be entertained, whichever I want."

"You get what you want most of the time, don't you?"

"Yes. I suspect you do, too, so it's annoying when we don't."

"We each intend to get what we want involving the ranch. Let's just hope we can move to a point where the outcome is mutually satisfying and fulfilling."

"I intend to do that, Caitlin," he said softly, and she had a feeling he wasn't talking about the ranch at all, but about making love.

In a short time they were airborne. She looked at his ranch below as they circled and headed southeast. "Tell me when we are no longer over your ranch."

He gazed outside and she studied his profile, looking at the firm jaw, his prominent cheekbones and symmetrical features. His thick brown hair was combed from his face. She was frustrated by her helplessness to sway Jake.

With his recent acquisitions of neighboring property, Jake's sprawling ranch was enormous. He couldn't possibly need all the land she saw below.

"There," he said, leaning close to her and pointing below. "Since I bought the Patterson place, that's the southeast boundary now. We're negotiating for wind turbines all along the land you see below."

She lost track of what he was saying. Jake was only inches from her as he moved closer to point out his holdings. His mouth was mere inches away, his thickly lashed eyes adding to his handsome appeal.

As if he realized her thoughts, he turned to look into her eyes and her heart thudded. Her breathing altered and she tilted her face up to his. When his gaze lowered to her mouth, her heartbeat pounded.

He leaned the last few inches to kiss her. His lips were warm, sensual, moving slowly on hers while his tongue slipped into her mouth.

She kissed him in return, steadily thinking no, no, no, yet unable to resist him. Desire heightened, her breathing altered. Jake was the most exciting man she had known.

His arm slipped around her waist and she placed a hand against his warm, solid chest, feeling his heart racing beneath her touch.

She kissed him until his arm tightened around her waist and she realized he might be moving her to his lap. He raised his head. "Unbuckle. I want to hold you."

His voice was deep, gravelly and desire filled his blue eyes that had darkened with passion. Her heart raced while she fought her own desire. She placed her hands on his arms.

"Jake, I won't look fit to go out for dinner if I move to your lap. We should stop this craziness anyway."

"It's not craziness," he answered quietly. "I want you, Caitlin." He looked her straight in the eye and barriers around her heart crumbled.

"Don't," she whispered, placing her fingertips lightly on his mouth, aware of his lips beneath her touch. "You can't become important to me, Jake."

"Just kisses—that's not earth-shattering."

She inhaled and bit back her answer. While his kisses had too strong an effect, she had no intention of admitting it to him.

"I'm going to go straighten my clothes. We're cruising now and I can move around according to the pilot."

As she walked away from him, she tingled, feeling certain he watched her. When she returned, she met his watchful gaze and this time had to get to her seat beneath his scrutiny.

He looked faintly amused, as if knowing that his kisses set her ablaze. "So there's no relationship with anyone right now," he said.

"No. I'm not into casual relationships. You said you won't marry. Well, I don't want anything casual. It's a fine thing we're not in each other's lives. It would not be a happy outcome."

"Most relationships begin casually," he said.

She shook her head. "Nothing I'm involved in because I have to have deep commitment. Which I've never had. Nothing has gone beyond the casual stage so far."

Frowning slightly, Jake framed her face. "Nothing? I find that impossible to imagine. I intend to get beyond the casual stage, Caitlin. I want to know you. I want you in my life. We have a mutual attraction that is spectacular. You feel it," he declared.

"Jake, I can't get closely involved with you. I'm not going to, just know that right now."

"We'll see," he said softly and she couldn't catch her breath. They were on the verge of kissing, only it was more volatile than before. She couldn't understand her escalating reaction to him, nor could she get rid of it.

She pulled away, gazing at him with what she hoped was a cool composed regard even while he sent her breathing and heartbeat into a scramble. "You keep your distance, Jake," she whispered. Her faint voice took all the demand out of her words.

"No," he replied. "I have no intention of keeping my distance because part of you doesn't want me at arm's length. Part of you wants to kiss and make love. You can't stop from revealing it."

With a sinking feeling, she looked away. He was right. He could easily demolish her resistance. How was she going to keep him under control and at arm's length all evening? Did she want to keep him at a distance? She wanted the old house and the people who had worked for her to stay on more than anything she had ever wanted since she was a small child. The house was a tie to all she loved in her childhood. The people deserved to be able to stay, not uprooted when they were becoming older.

Letting Jake into her life, succumbing to the fiery attraction might bind him to her strongly enough he would sell the place to her. It was like selling herself to get what she wanted, yet there was another argument. Jake was the sexiest man she had ever met. What would happen if she followed her desire and let a relationship develop?

She thought about her own life and her mother. That's what her mother had done and had an unwanted baby she had given up for adoption. Caitlin would never give up a baby, but she didn't want to bring one into the world fathered by a man who had no interest in a family or a commitment.

All her life she had vowed any relationship would have to be lasting, filled with love, not lust. What she and Jake had found was lust, spectacular, sizzling, but with no substance.

All through the flight, she flirted, enjoyed him and stewed about the outcome of the evening.

When they landed, a limo took them to a private club on the top floor of a tower in downtown Dallas.

They sat at a table in a secluded corner with a glowing candle centered on the table. Soft piano music played near the dance floor, while she barely noticed her surroundings. Her focus was Jake.

Desire built, increasing from the moment she had opened her front door to greet him. His kisses, his touches, his flirting, his declarations of how much he wanted her, all of it already had her shivering with need, thinking about his fiery kisses and anticipating being in his arms.

As she looked across the candlelight into his blue eyes, he reached out to take her hand. His fingers were larger, tan against her skin. Calluses on his palm were rough, making her wonder what he had done to cause them because he spent most of time in offices and in cities. When he was on the ranch, she couldn't imagine he did manual labor.

"I should look at the menu," she said, taking her gaze from him and reaching for the black menu that had been given to her.

During the time wine was poured and they ordered, conversation became impersonal, revolving around dinner choices and she relaxed.

"What's your next project, Caitlin? Will it take you away from Texas or Santa Fe?"

"No. I have appointments in Houston toward the end of October. I took plenty of time off because I've been working a long, intensive schedule the past two months and I've been in Europe taking pictures for a book project."

Steak and lobster dinners arrived. While they ate, she asked Jake about his life and childhood, discovering that he had lived on the ranch year-round the first six years of his life before the Bentons began to spend more time in Dallas.

After dinner Jake said, "Let's dance, Caitlin."

She nodded, standing when he took her hand, and they moved to the dance floor. She stepped into Jake's arms to dance to an old ballad. Jake was warm, tall, agile. Everything about him was appealing except the most important things: his family, his ownership of her home and ranch, his avoidance of commitment.

The contact from dancing with him fanned her desire. She wanted him and she was vulnerable. There hadn't been any man in her life in a long time and none she had ever been serious about. This fascination with Jake remained a constant danger to her well-being and her determination to avoid the wrong relationship.

When a fast number followed, their gazes locked while they danced. He was sexy, light on his feet and each touch sizzled, combating her efforts to cling to caution.

As he twirled her around, she turned to see blatant lust in his blue eyes. He wanted her and his desire made her heart drum. He pulled her tightly against him. "I want you, Caitlin," he whispered, saying what she could read in his eyes. He spun her away and she danced, feeling desired, seductive, knowing she was flirting with temptation again. The whole evening was building toward seduction, in an unwanted escalation of their relationship.

Later, slow dancing in his embrace while they barely moved around the dance floor, he whispered in her ear, "I have a condo here. Let's go there so we can have some privacy."

This was the moment to say no and go home. As she danced, held close against him, after a dream evening, she didn't want to say goodbye. As if watching a puppet in a play, she nodded. "Very well, Jake. For a while. I still want to fly back to the ranch."

"Whatever you want. All you have to do is tell me."

When the number ended, he took her hand and they returned to their table where she retrieved her purse.

"Now I can show you where I live in Dallas. We'll pass the office, too."

She was familiar with Dallas and had a general idea where they were going. When they reached a suburban area, Jake pointed to a twenty-story building on a business campus with a complex of buildings. "There's the Benton campus. We have a lot of diversification. I'm in the main building. Gabe is in the ten-story one next to the tallest building."

"Will you lose anything concerned with the business if you don't do what your dad wants in the coming year?"

"I'm risking all of this, although so far, Dad has simply threatened my inheritance and what he has in his will. I'm not worried. I'm setting up my own business. Dad can do what he wants."

"I can't believe you would give up such a fortune. You could marry and live the kind of life where you and your wife would never have to see each other."

"No. The day I marry, I will be so in love I can't think straight. I'm not ready for that. I haven't ever had a serious relationship or considered marriage and I'm not about to get into a shallow relationship to please my father. He can have his money, his business and everything else. I'll walk away still being my own person."

"That's amazing. You must have incredible willpower."

"Incredible stubbornness is what he'll call it. I don't care. Here's my condo," Jake said, turning into a gated area. He punched a code and tall iron gates swung inward.

Helping her out of the car, Jake took her arm. "I'll give you a brief tour," he said, leading her into a kitchen that made her ranch kitchen look the age it was. Dark wood was softened by the lighting and splashes of color in plants, jars and copper-bottomed pots. An adjoining sitting room was inviting with plaid-covered furniture.

The central hall held a fountain and pool. The living area

was another inviting room with leather furniture and walls of books. As Jake shed his coat and tie and unbuttoned the top buttons of his shirt, her mouth went dry and she forgot his condo.

He glanced at her, then focused more intently and she looked away, moving around the room to look at shelves holding books, vases and pictures. There were pictures of Jake with his brother and sister.

"Even though your father meddles in your life, you had a family with a brother and sister and that's wonderful."

"You at least had your grandmother."

"That I did and I had more in Cecilia, Altheda and Kirby who were like family to me. No, I will always be grateful for my grandmother who gave me a wonderful life."

"All evening I have wanted to do this," he said, reaching up to take the clip out of her hair. While locks tumbled on her shoulders, he placed the clip on a shelf and ran his fingers through her hair. His gaze held hers and it was difficult to get her breath again.

"This is the way I like you best."

Her heart drummed because he stood only inches from her. His gaze was on her mouth and his fingers still combed slowly through her hair. His arm circled her waist, drawing her closer and then he kissed her, his mouth covering hers while his tongue slipped into her mouth.

Her heart pounded. Unable to resist, she stood on tiptoe, put her arms around his neck to hug him as she kissed him in return. "This wasn't going to happen to me," she whispered, looking up at him and meeting blue eyes filled with desire.

"It's happened and it's fantastic," he said. "Stop fighting me and yourself."

"I don't think I've ever fought you," she whispered in return, lost in a spiral of yearning and hot kisses as she clung to him and returned his kisses.

Desire enveloped her, driving away all reason. She wanted only Jake, running her hands across his broad shoulders and feeling his warm skin beneath the fine cotton of his dress shirt. Then her fingers were at his buttons and she twisted them free to run her hands over his chest, tangling her fingers in his thick mat of chest hair.

He tightened his arm around her waist, kissing her hard while his other hand slipped down her back and over her bottom. She gasped as sensations bombarded her. He shifted while he tugged down the zipper of her dress.

Cool air brushed her heated skin, but she barely noticed, thinking about Jake and his kisses, his hard, muscled body pressed against hers, his sculpted chest.

She turned her head slightly. "Jake, I'm not going to complicate my life."

"Not asking you to," he replied while he kissed and caressed her. "Just kisses and touches, Caitlin."

But it wasn't just kisses and touches. He was more exciting, more intriguing. In addition to the attraction, she had gained respect for him from being with him and for his attitude toward his controlling father.

Each kiss was a link that strengthened her desire for him. The whisper of caution was gone as quickly as it had come.

She wanted to be in his arms, kissing him and being kissed by him. And if this was a way to get him to think about selling to her, so be it. She was not getting into an intimate relationship with him over the sale of land, but a few kisses—thoughts stopped plaguing her as she gave herself to the moment and kissed him with all her pent-up longing for him.

He lightly pushed her dress off her shoulders and it fell to her hips. While he kissed her, he unsnapped the wisp of lace that was her bra and his hand cupped her breast, his thumb caressing her.

She moaned with pleasure, wanting to caress him, to stir him as he stirred her. She tugged his shirt free and ran her hand over his rock-solid chest. Jake held her away to look at her, his gaze hot and hungry.

"So beautiful," he whispered, cupping her breasts and bending down to circle a taut bud with his tongue. She clung to his shoulders, closing her eyes and relishing his loving, wanting all of him, wanting a night of love with him and knowing it was forbidden.

Minutes, seconds, she didn't know. She groaned and stepped forward to embrace him, thrusting her hips against him, feeling his erection and knowing he was ready for love.

She clung to him tightly, kissing him long and hard, her tongue going deep and stroking his.

As he kissed her hungrily in return, his arm tightened around her. Her heart thudded against his and she could barely get her breath. She wanted all barriers between them gone.

Releasing her slightly, Jake pushed the dress off her hips and it fell to the floor around her ankles while his hand drifted down over her belly and lower between her thighs.

Moaning with pleasure and regret, she gripped his wrist and stopped him. "Jake," she whispered, gasping for breath. "We have to stop. I can't go into a night of love or anything casual and at this point, loving between us would be casual."

"I want to make love to you all night long," Jake whispered, caressing her and showering kisses on her throat and ear. "I want you in my arms in my bed."

While her heartbeat raced, she scooped up her dress, pulling it in place as he straightened to watch her.

Her heart still pounded from wanting him. His hair was tousled; his chest was bare, appealing and muscled with a faint sheen of sweat on his shoulders. He was aroused, ready, his trousers bulging with evidence. She longed to step back into his embrace, but a lifetime of promises to herself kept her from doing so.

"I'm not ready for casual loving. You're not ready for a commitment. I want you to take me home now."

He gazed at her without saying a word and she wondered what ran through his mind. Finally he nodded, reaching out to take her shoulders and turn her around. He pulled up the zipper on her dress and brushed a light kiss on her nape before turning her back around to face him.

"I'll take you back if that's what you absolutely want, but I've enjoyed being with you. You have tomorrow off and I have to be in Dallas tomorrow for two appointments. Let's stay here tonight. I have plenty of extra bedrooms and you'll have yours and I'll have mine. We can be together and tomorrow I'll make my appointments and then we'll fly back to the ranch. How will that be? Stay here tonight."

Six

One more time they would be thrown together in close contact, spending the night under the same roof. For her own well-being the answer should be no. Spending more time with him would make it harder to say no to his seduction. But it might make it more difficult for him to refuse to sell the land to her, so that meant a yes. The easiest answer.

She nodded. "I'd like that, actually."

"Let's go get something to drink and we can sit and talk where it's comfortable."

"Same as before, Jake, I don't have anything else to wear. I brought nothing with me."

He gave her a crooked grin. "Here, too, I'm prepared, although I could make a suggestion, but I don't think you'd take it."

"I can guess that suggestion," she remarked dryly, uncertain, but suspecting he was teasing. "No thanks. I'll take you up on what you have, which was very nice at the ranch."

"Great. Let's get something to drink. Cold or hot? Soft or otherwise?"

"I'll take a cup of hot tea."

"I'll pass on that one and have a cold beer."

She walked beside him down the hall, trying to get composed and ignore desire that was still white-hot and making her acutely aware of him, more sensitive than ever to the slightest physical contact with him. He had come so close to seduction—a few more minutes and she couldn't have said no. If they were together often, she wouldn't be able to continue to resist him.

"I have to be in Houston tomorrow night because I have an appointment early Tuesday morning."

"I'll get you back in time to go home. I have to be in Kansas City this week. I'll be gone until Friday. Go out with me again next Friday."

"Jake, what about the ranch? I thought we were going to talk tomorrow."

"I'll get an answer to you as soon as I can. I have people checking out the sale for me. Gabe brought information to me at the ranch. Just a little longer, Caitlin."

She studied him, wondering about the delay. She suspected if he wanted to buy it and she had it for sale, there would be no such delay, study of the situation or long thinking about it. She still thought he was stalling for a reason. So far only one reason came to mind—seduction. Now he had asked her out Friday night. Perhaps that was what he had been waiting for.

"How about Friday?" he asked, his dark gaze steady.

"I'll be in Houston, Jake. Not at the ranch."

"I'll pick you up in Houston and have something planned. Maybe a weekend in a tropical place. How's that?"

She smiled. "Extreme. What about dinner in Houston?"

"Far too short a time with you and too ordinary. Let's get away somewhere."

"Sounds exciting," she answered truthfully. "Very well. Let me know when you decide where, so I can let my friend Ginny know where I am. We keep track of each other because neither of us has a family any longer. Ginny's family had the McCorkin drugstore in town. Another kid you don't remember because you didn't pay any attention to her."

"Hey, you were little kids."

"I know. Actually, Cecilia and I talk every day and she keeps track of me, too."

"I'll give you an itinerary. Tracie, my secretary, will send you a text."

"I'll look forward to Friday," she said, knowing she would and at the same time, she would worry about his decision and wonder when she would hear. She didn't expect to hear from him until after their weekend together because she still felt he was procrastinating while he hoped to seduce her.

"You're quiet, Caitlin. What are you thinking?"

"I'm wondering how I'll be able to resist you the next time."

He turned to face her and desire still burned in his expression. "I hope to hell you can't. I want you. I can't sleep for thinking about you. You're special, more exciting than any other woman I've known. I hope you feel that way about me."

Her pulse jumped with his admission. At the same time his words locked around her heart, tugging on her. He waited for an answer from her, staring intently at her.

"You know you excite me," she whispered. "You came into my life like a whirlwind and you'll go out like one. I want my heart in one piece when that happens."

"I came into your life when I drove home. You were the

storm waiting to break. I don't know that I'll be gone in a flash. Not since every minute with you gets more interesting. There are some times in life you have to take a chance."

"This isn't one of them. That's what my mother did and the consequences were disastrous."

"You don't have to repeat what happened to your mother. We're different people. I'm not Titus Santerre and you're not your mother. Besides, it brought you and your grandmother together."

"We're arguing uselessly," she said, waving her hand.

He turned to head for the kitchen again and she walked beside him. "It'll set my parents back to know we've gone out together."

"What about your feelings for your sister?" she asked.

"That was different and a terrible time for all of us. My mom detests Will and your dad. I doubt if she has strong feelings about you or your grandmother except they always snubbed each other in town."

"I know that. I lived with Grandmother."

"Crazy family feud," he said. "Maybe we can end it."

"You don't really mean that."

"Sure I do," he said as he heated water for her tea, then got out his cold beer and snapped open the bottle. He got a cup and saucer and a small tray, placing everything on it.

"Let's sit on the sofa. It'll be more comfortable than at the table," he said, motioning toward the adjoining sitting room. She sat and tucked her legs beneath her while he placed the teapot on a table near the sofa. He sipped his cold beer.

"What's your friend Ginny do? I guess the McCorkins still run the drugstore."

"Yes, they do. Her dad always says he'll never retire. He has a big pharmacy and that's what he mostly does. Ginny is a drug rep in Houston for a pharmaceutical company."

"That's easy to figure. She grew up knowing those people. She has the background."

"She studied to be a pharmacist, but she likes sales."

Jake nodded. "Where do you get your clients? I guess now, it's easy, but at first, how did you get them?"

"It's never been hard. People see my photographs and ask me about them and want me to take their pictures. I've been fortunate."

"Plus a few other things. I know about being fortunate. Do you have many employees at your galleries and shop?"

"About eight run the galleries. I have an office staff, my secretary, my accountant, a sales manager—just a small staff of people."

"I'll have to go to Houston, see your office and your gallery there. How about showing me sometime soon? I can fly us there."

"Of course. Whenever you want," she answered, willing to do so, yet thinking it would probably never happen and he was just talking. Perhaps if he sold her the land, but she wouldn't allow herself to speculate on what she would do if she got what she wanted from him. "I don't think it will be so spectacular to you."

"I'll be the judge of that. Did your grandmother see your success?"

"Yes, she saw the success I've had and she was pleased. I have some wonderful pictures of her because she was always happy to pose for me."

"Sorry you lost her."

She squeezed his hand in thanks. "Did you go to work for your dad right out of college?"

"For one year. The next year I switched to a different company because I wanted experience that I wouldn't get in our company. Two years later I was a vice president of that company and then I acquired a small company of my own

The year after that, Dad wanted me to come back. He was getting ready to retire and wanted me in the family empire and made me an offer I couldn't refuse," Jake said. "I've been there since and I'll stay."

"You sound as if you're happy with your work."

"Very. Speaking of going to work—when I go in the morning, is there anything you need to do in Dallas?"

"There are things I can do," she replied. "Catch up on my emails, my calls, go check out some photographic equipment here."

"If you stay here, there's a pool you can use. You can swim, spend a leisurely morning, work out in the exercise room. Do whatever you want to do. I have an appointment at the office and some papers to sign. I'm talking to our geologist about your ranch. Then I'll be back and we can go to lunch."

"Whatever you and your geologists and anyone else decide about oil, wind, water, gas—whatever on our land—that has nothing to do with what I want, Jake. You've met Cecilia and Kirby and Altheda. They're hanging on your decision."

"They may have to hang just a bit longer. I don't want to rush this. Selling back the house isn't what I planned."

A chill slithered down her middle. She couldn't contemplate that he wouldn't capitulate and let her buy back some land. For the first time she realized he was taking his time and keeping her dangling. If and when he refused—in that minute, she would be out of his life. Was he stringing her along because he wanted seduction? The question still plagued her because that seemed the only possible answer.

"Don't look at me as if I just became a two-headed monster."

"You almost have," she said. "I just can't understand the delay in making this decision. You don't run your businesses in this manner."

"I don't make snap decisions often," he remarked dryly.

She realized she was arguing with him and possibly making him dig his heels in—and the sale less likely. She swirled her tea slightly, knowing she should let go of it and give him time.

He covered her hand with his. "Stop worrying. I'll give you a decision within a few days."

She smiled at him, but it was an effort and her heart was not in it. She suspected it showed.

He tilted up her chin. "You have the most beautiful green eyes, Caitlin," he said. "I'm sure you've been told that before."

"Thank you. I'm glad you think so," she said, aware of the casual touch of his fingers on her chin, yet it made her tingle.

"Why haven't I seen you in the intervening years? You lived at your grandmother's house during your college years didn't you?" he asked. He caught a long lock of her hair and twisted it in his fingers. She felt the faint tugs on her scalp, little pulls that should be nothing, yet were tingling and stirred her smoldering desire. She tried to ignore his fingers combing through her hair, but it was impossible to ignore anything about him.

"Yes, but I wasn't home that often and I doubt if you were, either. You wouldn't have seen me on the ranch, only in town. After I was grown if you had seen me, you wouldn't have recognized me."

"True enough, but I would have noticed you and probably asked someone who you were."

Reminding her that he was all about *attraction*. "You told me you want to make money in the future. What else in your future, Jake? What do you want when you already have everything you want in life?" she said, hoping to change the subject and get him talking about himself while she regained her composure.

"I definitely do not have everything I want," he said with an emphasis on *everything* that made it personal, as if referring to their lovemaking.

"I would guess there are few times you don't get what you want at this point in your life."

"True. If I want something, I hope to get it."

Again, she thought the last was aimed at her and their lovemaking. "Noble ambition," she said, keeping the conversation impersonal.

"And in particular," he said, his voice dropping, "I want to make love to you, Caitlin, to finish what we started tonight. And sometime we will," he added with conviction in his voice. His words were a caress, as electrifying as a touch of his fingers.

"Maybe, Jake. Just maybe. There are too many outside factors."

"I intend to keep you in my life if I possibly can."

"You know one way to do so." She was aware of her own power over him. It was as ruthless as using the ranch for leverage to seduce her. "It's really simple."

"Simple. And not so simple. Just trust that I'm working on it."

It was all she'd get from him until he made his decision. She tried to stop thinking about it. His fingers lightly caressed her nape, a feathery touch that was erotic, stirring desire even more.

She sipped hot tea and tried to concentrate on his conversation and ignore the clamoring of her body or his hand wreaking havoc with her. He was driving away all hope of a peaceful night.

As she talked to him, her voice got a breathlessness that he had to notice. Desire burned in the depths of his blue eyes. On one level they were sitting, chatting, getting to know each other. On another level, Jake was still working his seduction with each slight caress.

"What hobbies do you have?" she asked. "You've told me about skiing, swimming, things you like to do."

"There's not much of anything right now because work has been demanding."

"I remember seeing you in rodeos. You were a bronc rider and I think a few times I've seen you bull riding."

"I did a little bull riding, but stopped when I hurt my shoulder. I did bronc riding and calf roping for a long time. Gabe and I did the calf roping."

She listened to him talk about his rodeo days, horses he had owned and they compared notes on horses.

They talked about their college days, growing up on the neighboring ranches. In all their conversation, they avoided mentioning the family feud, as well as any talk about the future.

She finally noticed the time. "Jake, it's two in the morning. I should go to bed."

"Sure," he said, standing. When she reached for her empty cup, he shook his head.

"Leave it. Someone will get it tomorrow."

"A housekeeper comes in?"

"Yes. You'll meet him in the morning. I won't leave until long after you're up. I work out early in the morning and swim a lap in the pool. You can join me swimming or go in later."

"I don't have a suit."

"There are new suits in the drawer. I'll show you. You can find something you can wear, I'm sure."

"You're well equipped for a woman to sleep over," she remarked, wondering how many times he had had to furnish things for his overnight female guests.

"It's easy to keep extras on hand. I have a lot of company and my staff takes care of the needed items. I don't deal with it at all. Also, there are straw bags in the closet. Whatever clothes you wear, just toss in a bag and take them with you because the next person won't want something worn by someone else. I don't keep anything someone has worn."

"That's nice, but you sound as if you have a habit of guests sleeping over."

"Not really. I'm just prepared for company. Sometimes guys stop by and then stay to hunt. Female friends have stayed, married couples. A lot of my friends drop by the ranch because they know they're welcome."

At the door of her room she turned to tell him good-night. Jake's arm banded her waist and he drew her close as he bent down to kiss her. His mouth came down on hers possessively. He wrapped her in his embrace and kissed her, sending her heartbeat racing.

Circling her arms around his neck, she clung to him, wanting him with scalding desire, fighting the pull, unable to break off the kiss that deepened. She was lost, spinning away in a fiery blaze of passion. She combed her fingers through the short hair at the back of his head, holding him tightly, wanting the barriers of clothing away. That was no solution to her problem. Instead, it would only create bigger complications in her life.

She kissed him, returning passion, wanting to melt him and make him hunger for her and try to please her. She refused to fall into his arms completely, to be easy and vulnerable and worse yet, have her heart hostage to him.

"Jake," she whispered, breaking off the kiss. "I can't complicate my life. Good night," she said, slipping out of his arms and entering her room to close the door. She leaned against it, her heart pounding while she gasped for breath. She had seen his heavy-lidded expression, lust clearly consuming him. He wanted her physically no matter how he felt toward her otherwise.

She had no illusions that he had lost his animosity toward her family. Probably not altogether toward her. His deep dislike of Santerres lay smoldering beneath the surface of his friendly facade. She hadn't lost her own feelings regarding the Bentons. They had altered slightly because she liked Jake, but he was a Benton and the Bentons had done some bad things to Santerres through the years. The feud hadn't died completely. It never would between Jake and Will, even if he sold to her, but selling her home to her would go a long way toward mending fences.

She didn't want to think about the possibility that he wouldn't sell the house back to her.

She moved around the room and then began looking for the clothing he had said was available. She found new clothing wrapped in tissue, including a silk nightgown. As she changed, she was once again amazed that she was spending another night beneath the same roof as Jake.

When ready for bed, she found a book on the shelf that looked interesting and she curled up to read because sleep wasn't going to come for a while longer. Her body still tingled and she couldn't get Jake and their date out of mind. In minutes she climbed in bed, switched off the light and thought about Jake.

The next morning when she entered the kitchen, she was dressed in blue cotton slacks and a matching shirt that had been in the assortment of new clothing on hand. She wore her high-heeled sandals and had put her hair in one long braid.

As she entered the dining area, Jake stood. He pulled out a chair and his gaze assessed her quickly. "You look fresh and beautiful."

"Thank you. You look quite handsome yourself," she said, taking in Jake's charcoal business suit, dress shirt and tie. "I met your housekeeper as I came through the kitchen."

"Ah, Fred. He's an excellent cook as you'll see. I have an appointment in downtown Dallas. If you want, you can ride in with me. I moved it a little later so we can ride in together. Then you can have my driver take you wherever you'd like to go."

"Fine," she said, thinking of tasks she could do with time and the resources in Dallas.

"Remember, I need to get back to the ranch today. I have a rental car to return and I have to go to Houston tomorrow."

"And I have to leave town, too."

She ate breakfast with him, hearing more stories about the ranch and answering his questions about her business and life in Houston.

Finally they rode to town in a long black limousine driven by a man named Scotty. She told Jake goodbye and then asked Scotty to drive her to a photography shop. Scotty waited patiently while she spent an hour discussing equipment with one of the salesmen. She bought some necessary items and finally went to a shopping center where Scotty waited while she purchased some clothing. When she climbed back into the limousine, she had shed the clothing she had gotten from Jake and was wearing new green silk slacks and a matching shirt.

At two they picked up Jake and within the hour, they were airborne, heading back to the ranch in West Texas.

Jake drove her back to her house, and as always, her heart squeezed at the sight of the old Victorian she'd grown up in. He walked her to the door, and she turned to face him. "Please think about selling the house to me and remember, it means the world to me. I never dreamed Will would sell without letting me know. If I had known, I would have kept up with what he was doing."

"I know how much you want the place. But you don't live here, Caitlin. If I don't sell it back to you—for *business* reasons—I'll see to it that the residents have comfortable places to go. I won't put anyone out in the cold."

She ran her hand along the beveled glass in the door. "I explained that we all have the means to live elsewhere quite comfortably, Jake. We love this place. I know one shouldn't be so attached to a place, but I guess my roots are here." She had a knot in her throat and couldn't bear to think that he wouldn't sell. "I don't see why you have to hang on to this little patch of land, Jake. I really don't. It's important to several of us, but it means nothing to you. I can't even talk about tearing down this old home."

"Stop worrying. I haven't said I wouldn't sell." He frowned slightly. "Just give me the time I asked for, Caitlin, to make a decision."

"I have no choice in the matter," she said, hating the flat tone of her voice, but unable to hide her emotions where the house was concerned.

"You have some choices," he said quietly, his arm banding her waist as he bent to kiss her. His tongue thrust into her mouth and her worries and fears were pushed away. Anger, desire, determination replaced them. She wanted to melt his resistance, storm the barriers of his heart that he kept so closed away. She wrapped her arms around his neck and kissed him in return, responding fully, thrusting her hips against him.

He groaned as his fingers wound in her hair. She could feel tugs on her scalp until her braid was half undone. Raking his fingers through her hair, he pulled locks free. He leaned over her kissing her while his hand lightly caressed her breast. He raised his head. "Where's your door key?"

As she handed it to him, he continued kissing her. In a moment he walked her backward into her house and kicked the door closed behind them. She heard the key fall to the floor while they still kissed.

"Cecilia and Altheda?" he paused to ask.

"They're sound asleep in another wing of the house. They're never in here at night," she answered and he pulled her close again. As he kissed her, he walked her into the nearest room and closed the door.

In seconds Jake pushed her blouse off her shoulders. While he continued kissing her, he unfastened the clasp of her bra and shoved it away to cup her breasts. His hands were warm, his thumbs circling her nipples making her moan with pleasure. "Jake," she whispered as she ran her hands over his shoulders. She wanted him and each kiss only inflamed desire. He was forbidden, dangerous to her future, desirable beyond all dreams.

She twisted free the buttons of his shirt to run her fingers through the thick mat of hair on his chest.

When his hands went to her slacks and they fell around her ankles, she raised her head. He watched her, his eyes half-lidded, burning with desire that mirrored her own feelings.

"I'm not going to complicate my life. We can't make love."

"Yes, we can," he whispered, caressing her breasts, cupping them in his hands again as he bent down to take one in his mouth, his tongue stroking her. She gasped with pleasure and ran her fingers through his hair, momentarily yielding to the sensual delight before she stopped him and shook her head.

"No," she whispered.

"You're gorgeous," he told her as he caressed her. His touch was feathery, setting her ablaze. She trembled with wanting him. In spite of that, she was determined there would be no seduction.

"Jake, that's enough. I cannot complicate my life. I won't do it."

She pulled her clothing in place, aware he watched her. He

stood in silence with smoldering fires in his gaze. When she was dressed, she faced him.

He gazed at her for a moment. "I'll pick you up in Houston Friday night about six. Send me your address. I have your phone number. I'll talk to you this week."

"Thanks for a wonderful time."

He framed her face with his hands. "Sometime, Caitlin, you won't send me away, you'll be mine," he said solemnly.

"You want me, Jake, but when I go out of your life, it won't take long for you to forget me."

"You're not going out of my life anytime soon," he said gruffly. All his words were as searing as his caresses. She responded to everything, wanting to be back in his embrace, to kiss him. "Sometime, you'll want me to make love to you, to hold you and kiss you as much as I want."

"I already do," she whispered and saw his eyes flicker. "But we're not going there, Jake. You know why I won't. It's been a wonderful time with you. Good night."

He gazed her for another tense moment before he brushed a light kiss on her lips and left, closing the door behind him. She didn't follow him out. She locked the door and headed for her bedroom, knowing she would have one more night where sleep wouldn't come and when it did it would be filled with dreams of Jake.

Jake drove to his ranch and took the plane back to Dallas. He had a busy week ahead in Kansas City. It was almost dawn when he stretched out in bed. He wanted to call Caitlin, just to talk to her, but each time he reached for his phone, he paused and then put it back on the table.

He should leave her alone. They were getting too close. He had wanted to seduce her while he still barely knew her, but now, he was getting to know her, enjoying being with her. She impressed him with her photography, her poise, her determination. She was becoming more than just a gorgeous, desirable woman he might get into his bed. He didn't want to become fast friends or get too close. It would hurt her more when he turned her down for the sale.

He reached again for the phone and his hand stilled. He wanted to talk to her. He already missed her and her sunny laughter, her humor, her perception. Reluctantly, he had to admit that she would be furious and she would be hurt by his refusal to sell to her. He was beginning to really hate the prospect of hurting her. Should he rethink selling?

He surprised himself that he would even give the idea consideration. Here was his chance to get all Santerres out of West Texas for once and for all. He had intended to hold the land and refuse to sell to Caitlin. Yet why was it such a worrisome victory?

"Dammit," he said aloud in his dark bedroom. He tossed restlessly. Caitlin was twenty-eight, talented, gorgeous. She would probably fall in love and marry soon and that would be the end of the Santerre name in Texas anyway, because Will had told him he never was coming back since after selling the ranch, he could afford to live wherever he wanted.

The thought of Caitlin marrying wasn't a satisfying prospect, either. Jake refused to dwell on that speculation because he was the only man in her life at present so no marriage loomed on her horizon.

He missed her. Disgusted, he stared into the dark and thought about telling her that he wasn't going to sell her home back to her. Why was that becoming such an odious, distasteful chore? He didn't want to look closely at the answer to his own question. The old Victorian was one of the few ties she had to someone in her life. She had rejection on all sides except from her grandmother and those people who worked for Madeline Santerre. Why wouldn't Caitlin fight to keep that memory and keep close the people who had meant so much to her growing up?

Jake swore softly under his breath. He was beginning to feel like a villain in the whole picture. It was his land to do with as he pleased. There was no valid reason to sell to a Santerre whose house and animals would be in the way if Gabe brought in oil. *Tell her no the next time he was with her and be done with it.*

He silently vowed he would do it. Could he put her off long enough to get another weekend with her? He couldn't keep seeing her or he would *have* to sell to her. He shouldn't wait because the thought of refusing her was giving him growing qualms and guilt.

Despite promising to get back to her about her request this week, he decided he would make a business appointment to see her a week from Monday at her office so he could leave as soon as he told her. He owed it to her to tell her in person. If he didn't seduce her next weekend—and it looked as if she was going to continue to hold him at arm's length—he would tell her anyway.

The idea of Caitlin going out of his life at this point was totally unsatisfactory. He didn't want that to happen and the minute he refused to sell to her, she would be gone. He groaned, thinking it might be easier just to sell her the house and land she wanted and let her stay. If he did, she might be willing to make love with him.

He had to see his father tomorrow and he dreaded the meeting because they would probably get into another battle over marriage and his inheritance.

Jake made a mental note to call Tony and Gabe to set up lunch plans. They would cheer him up. He glanced at the clock again and wondered how early he could call Caitlin. Yesterday, she hadn't joined him in the kitchen until half past seven, so she must sleep late in the mornings.

Groaning, Jake turned to try to go to sleep, thinking about Caitlin and wanting her in his arms. If at all possible, he would see her again Friday night for a weekend getaway. This time he was going to kiss away all her objections. First, he had to get through another tedious session with his father.

Seven

At eight Jake arrived at the palatial mansion where he had grown up. He greeted the staff as he passed through the back hallway, the large family room, and entered the kitchen.

Trying to remember to hang on to his patience, Jake entered the breakfast room where his father sat in a maroon velvet robe while he read the morning paper and sipped what was probably his third cup of coffee. Dirk Benton was a man of habits and for all mornings Jake could recall, as long as his father was home, he rose at six, worked out for thirty minutes, showered and then went to the kitchen for breakfast which year after year was two eggs, toast, bacon and four cups of coffee while he read the morning newspaper. Jake was certain his mother, a late sleeper, was still upstairs.

"Good morning," Jake said.

Blue eyes focused on him as his father lowered the newspaper. "Good morning. Want breakfast? I know we have plenty."

"No thanks, I've already eaten. I brought some papers for you to sign," Jake said, sitting to the right of his father and opening a briefcase to withdraw a folder. He removed a pen from the briefcase and gave his father a quick refresher on what was involved.

Jake waited quietly while his father signed and then put everything back into the briefcase.

"What's your schedule this week?" Dirk asked.

"I'll be in Kansas City the rest of the week."

"Gabe is off to North Dakota later today. Your mother is going shopping in San Antonio. I'll be rather bored. Who did you take out this past weekend? Anyone we know?"

"As a matter of fact, it was someone you know. Better than I do," Jake said, for a moment enjoying the prospect of seeing his father's reaction. "Caitlin Santerre."

Dirk Benton's eyes narrowed while he inhaled sharply. "A Santerre? Will left town and you own their land. What are you doing going out with a Santerre? It has to be the granddaughter Madeline Santerre raised. Dammit, Jake, what the hell were you doing? Don't get tangled up with a Santerre the way Brittany did with Will."

Jake couldn't keep from enjoying his father's reaction. Let the old man stew a moment with the thought that Jake might be thinking of marrying a Santerre to get even for the demand that he marry or be disinherited.

"She was at the ranch when I got there last Saturday. She wants me to sell a little piece of her grandmother's ranch back to her. Will Santerre never let her know he was selling the place."

"Will Santerre is a selfish bastard. Actually that girl is the bastard child. Titus Santerre never wanted to claim her, but Madeline stepped in and adopted her and gave her the Santerre name. I'm not surprised about Will. He wouldn't care what she wanted. I'm sure he wouldn't share a nickel with her if he didn't have to according to Titus's will."

One of his father's eyebrows arched sharply and he studied Jake. "You're not selling it back to her, are you?"

"Of course not. She doesn't want any rights, just the old house and barn and the land they're on. She's sentimental about the house and wants the people who worked for Madeline to be able to live on the ranch for the rest of their lives."

"Well, you don't run a charity. So you told her no."

"Not yet. I will next week. I enjoyed going out with her," he stated honestly.

Dirk's eyes narrowed again. "Don't you marry her out of spite because I demanded you marry. That would be cutting off your nose to spite your face—as the old saying goes."

"No. I won't marry Caitlin Santerre. You can relax on that one. I am not marrying anyone this year."

"You'll come around to my way of thinking before the year's out and a fortune slips through your fingers. Otherwise, you'll regret your actions for the rest of your life."

"I can tell you now—I will not marry. I'll get along."

"Gabe can't give you the share you'll forfeit when he inherits it all."

"Dad, stop meddling in my life. Let me live my life in my own way. I'm not going to change my life because of your threats. Have you told Mom this latest one?"

"Yes. She knows you'll come around."

"You mean you told her that I'll come around and marry and not to worry. Well, you will see at the end of the year when I'm still not married. If I fell in love, I wouldn't marry. I won't be coerced into matrimony to suit my father. You might as well get accustomed to that notion. I better go. I have appointments this morning."

Dirk frowned. "Don't get too involved with a Santerre.

They are bad blood and bad for Bentons. Tell her you won't sell and stop going out with her. She'll cause you trouble one way or another, Jake."

"I'll remember. I think I'm going to be the one to cause her trouble this time. I'll see you, Dad," Jake said. He left, glad to get out of the house, thankful he could put distance between himself and his father.

Jake drove to the office and spent the morning so busy he forgot his dad and the thought of telling Caitlin he wouldn't sell to her. He couldn't forget Caitlin's beautiful face or lush body, though, and several times stopped what he was doing to think about holding her in his arms until he realized time was passing and he was lost in thought.

Midmorning he called her and talked briefly about nothing in particular. At noon, just as he approached the restaurant where he would meet his brother and his friends, he talked briefly to Caitlin again.

Tony, Nick and Gabe were already seated, drinking tall glasses of iced tea.

"Did you see Dad this morning?" Gabe asked as soon as Jake had ordered.

"Yep. He was his usual demanding self. It gave him a shock to learn about Caitlin."

"Did he say anything to you about getting married?" Gabe asked.

"Deal is still on. He's certain I'll marry within this year."

"I hope to hell my dad doesn't try this ploy," Tony said. "Even as big a control freak as he is, I can't imagine him demanding that I marry within the year. I don't know that he's that eager for me to marry anyway."

"I hope Dad doesn't try this one on me," Gabe said. "I can't do what you're doing, Jake. I don't even want to think about it."

"I'm not marrying to please him. There's only one reason to

marry—you have to be crazy in love. You were just fortunate, Nick."

"Damn fortunate to have found Grace. Dad's been gloriously happy with two grandchildren. He hasn't tried to tell me to do anything since he learned he would have two grandchildren. They take all his attention. You guys might think about that one," he said and the others laughed.

"I told Tony and Nick about Caitlin Santerre," Gabe said, sipping tea and crunching a small piece of ice.

"She must really want to keep her family home," Tony remarked. "Will Santerre was always bad news."

"How'd she take your refusal to sell to her?" Gabe asked.

"I haven't told her yet," Jake replied and Gabe's eyebrows shot up as his eyes widened.

"Why not?"

"I'm going out with her this next weekend. I figure as soon as I tell her, I've seen the last of her. I had a fun time with her."

"That's amazing," Gabe said. "A Benton and a Santerre out together. Of course, Will and Brittany went out together."

"Is she good-looking?" Tony asked and Jake gave him a look.

"That's what I figured," Tony answered. "She must be damned gorgeous."

"So when will you tell her?" Gabe persisted.

"A week from now. I know I can't keep putting her off. I'll have to give her an answer."

"She'll be bitter, but I can't imagine her causing you trouble. Now if you were dealing with Will, no telling what kind of grief he would try to cause. The fight would be back on between the Bentons and the Santerres."

"No, she won't cause trouble. At least I don't think so."

To his relief, conversation moved away from his problems

and they talked about business, about the next basketball game. Later, Gabe turned to Jake.

"Did you tell Dad about going out with a Santerre?"

"Yes, and you know his reaction. I ought to marry her out of spite, but I'm not giving him the satisfaction of a marriage, even one he doesn't like."

"I don't know when you got so stubborn," Gabe said.

"I'm not a kid and I'm getting tired of his interference."

"Amen to that one," Gabe said, pushing back his chair. "I've got to run. I have an appointment in thirty minutes and then I fly to Dakota. See y'all soon." He left, his long legs carrying him out quickly.

Nick placed a tip on the table. "I need to get going, too, Jake. Rethink turning down your dad. That's a huge fortune to pass on just to get satisfaction. There are millions of ways to get compensation if you get your dad's inheritance."

Jake shook his head. "I'll survive. Millionaire instead of billionaire. That's not a bad life. I have had it with his taking charge of what I do."

"Nothing will give you independence the same way inheriting your dad's fortune will," Tony remarked after Nick had gone. "As for Caitlin Santerre, that one should be easy. Tell her no deal, and she's gone forever. End of problem." Tony stood. "I should go now, too."

"I'll go with you," Jake said, leaving a tip before walking out with Tony.

"Guess I'll see you two weeks from now for basketball, right?" Tony asked.

"Sure. Usual time."

Jake headed to his car to drive to the office. *As for Caitlin Santerre, that one should be easy. Tell her no deal, and she's gone forever. End of problem.* Tony's words rang in his ears… *gone forever.* Jake didn't care. It couldn't be any other way with Caitlin, but he wanted to seduce her first. The thought of making love to her made him hot, aroused. He was leaving for Kansas City and he couldn't see her until the weekend. She'd go, because he still hadn't given her an answer, putting her off one more time. Friday night, he wanted to kiss her into losing all caution. Friday night—he was already looking forward to the evening with her.

Caitlin studied her image in the full-length mirror while her thoughts were filled of memories of Jake and his kisses. Excitement kept her tingly. Another weekend with Jake. It had been four long days since she had told him goodbye. And though her work and appointments had kept her very busy, she'd never stopped thinking about him. They had talked on the phone each day and every night. Every hour she chatted with him forged a tighter bond. Was it the same for him?

This week he would finally tell her his decision. He'd finally made a definite appointment for her to come in to his office in Dallas on Monday morning.

She still wondered whether he was holding out for this weekend with her before telling her he would not sell to her. Otherwise, why wouldn't he just tell her now?

Jake moved in exalted business circles with mega-deals. She couldn't imagine he had any trouble getting information about the Santerre ranch from his staff. Every hour of the past week had strengthened her guess that he would not sell.

She straightened the skirt of her red crepe dress. This one had a high neck, long sleeves and a skirt that came below her calves, with slits on either side of the straight skirt that revealed glimpses of her legs. She wore high-heeled matching sandals. Her hair was pinned up and she hoped she looked sophisticated, cool and poised. She didn't want Jake to see how much effect he could have on her so easily. Since they were in Houston, she had no idea what they would do. Stay here? Go to some close tropical place for the evening?

The doorbell rang and her pulse jumped at the mere prospect of seeing him again.

She hurried to the door to open it. The jump in her pulse when the doorbell chimed was nothing compared to the thud of her heart at the sight of him. She wanted to walk into his arms and kiss him. Instead, she smiled, while noticing the approval in his expression as he looked at her. How could she guard her heart against the handsome, commanding charmer who looked at her as if she were one of the greatest sights he'd ever seen?

She would have to remind herself almost every minute of the night that Jake was a Benton, an enemy and a threat to the well-being of her heart. In spite of that knowledge, she was breathless.

Tonight she was committed to spending the evening with him. She just had to remember that beneath the handsome facade was a tiger.

"You look gorgeous."

"Thank you. Come in while I get my purse."

Stepping into the entryway, he closed the door and reached for her. "Caitlin," he said in a husky voice that was its own warm caress. "Come here. It's been too long without you."

"Jake, it can't be—" she started. Her words ended abruptly when she saw the fires in his blue eyes. He drew her into his embrace swiftly, his mouth covering hers. She stepped into his arms, willing, eager. Clinging to him, she returned his passionate kiss.

"Damn, I missed you," he whispered, raising his head slightly and then coming back to kiss her again. She closed her eyes and gave herself to hungry kisses, wanting to agree with him that it had been too long, that she had missed him terribly, but she held back the words because they shouldn't be said to him. They could only lead to more heartbreak later.

They kissed until they were both out of breath, their hearts pounding. She could feel the beat of his heart as he held her tightly.

Finally, she stopped the kiss. "Jake, we must—"

"Shh. I had to kiss you. That's all I've thought about all week," he admitted. Her heart drummed and she stood on tiptoe to kiss him again. How else could she react after what he just said to her?

She didn't know how much time passed, but finally she stopped again. "Jake, you made plans for the evening."

"I can ditch them," he said in a gravelly voice. She shook her head.

"No. Let's not do that. I've told you, I'm not into seduction."

"You kiss like you are," he replied instantly and his statement took her breath.

"I missed you, too, but I want to go on with your dinner plans. Let me get my purse."

He followed her into the living area where she picked up her purse. When she turned, he was looking around the room.

"Very nice, Caitlin. Are these your pictures?" he asked, looking at framed black-and-whites of a bridge in Central Park, of the Grand Canyon, of a whale. He moved on to another wall with a grouping of pictures of people of various ages in different settings.

"I'm impressed. You're very good, but then I already knew that."

"Thanks." She glanced around the contemporary living area that had blue walls, with white furniture and touches of red in decorative pillows. "My place is a different style from yours."

"That makes life interesting," he said. "And entirely unlike the ranch house you love so much," he added.

"I like the change and this works for me. I still love the ranch house just the way it is."

"I'm surprised you don't try to duplicate it in your own place since you love it so much."

"No. That style belongs there and this change is satisfying, as well."

"That's surprising. So shall we leave now for New Orleans? Flying time is short and we can have a fun evening."

"Absolutely," she said, smiling at him over the thought of being in New Orleans for the evening.

She locked up and they got into his black limousine.

Jake reached over to take her hand and hold it in his. His fingers were warm, strong.

"New Orleans is one of my favorite places," she said.

"Next time I'll find a place you've never been before."

"New Orleans lends itself to fantastic snapshots and interesting people to photograph. Some of my favorite shots were taken in New Orleans. You ought to let me take your picture. You'd be an expressive subject."

"Expressive?" he asked, sounding amused. "So what shows in my face?"

"Wealth, arrogance—"

He chuckled. "Neither wealth nor arrogance can show in a face. Now if you take all of me and my suit, shoes, handmade monogrammed shirt—that's different."

"Just your face. They show. You've got that in-command-of-your-part-of-the-world expression in your eyes and the lift of your chin. It shows, Jake. A zest for life softens the harshness of the other two."

"Ridiculous, Caitlin. You see all that because you know me."

"If you'll let me take your picture, I'll show you someday. I know what people's faces usually reveal."

"We'll make a bet on the outcome. Make it worthwhile because I intend to win," he said.

"You're so sure of yourself," she said, amused by his smug tone. "That's what will show in your photograph."

"I've had a lot of photographs taken of myself and I can't recall ever thinking those attributes show."

"Of course, they won't to you. A bet—I'll think about that one."

They were soon airborne again on his private jet and just as he'd said, it was early evening when they arrived in New Orleans.

As they stepped out of the limo in the warm air of the French Quarter, the low wail of a trumpet by a street player assailed her, the sounds of people laughing and talking while four sailors passed them, turning to look briefly at her, then at Jake and away.

Jake whisked her inside a restaurant in a building that she was certain was well over one hundred years old. A maître d' greeted Jake and led them through a busy, darkened restaurant with soft lighting, blues being played. They passed a small dance floor with the band playing blues. The music became muted slightly as they followed the maître d'. They emerged onto an empty patio with one table set with white linen, a candle in a hurricane class encircled by a doughnut-shaped crystal vase holding gardenia blooms. Banks of pink oleanders, ferns, tall trees with hanging wisps of Spanish moss formed a border to the patio, enclosing it, giving them privacy while flickering torches furnished the lighting.

"Jake, this is beautiful," she said. "No one else is seated out here," she said when she was alone with him at their table

"I've reserved the patio for us tonight. We'll be undisturbed."

"This is all ours," she said, looking around again. "It's gorgeous out here."

"I agree about gorgeous," he said, gazing intently at her and her attention returned to him.

"You look ravishing tonight, Caitlin," he said in a deeper voice.

"Thank you," she answered, her pulse racing as it had since he had come to her door. "Do you have a condo here? Is this another night you'll want me to stay over until tomorrow?"

"I don't have a condo here. I rent a hotel suite. As far as staying over—that, Caitlin, is up to you."

Another tingle taunted her while his blue eyes held unmistakable desire. "Want a glass of wine?"

"Yes," she said, looking at the wine menu and trying to focus on words in front of her, anything to tear her gaze from his. He saw too much. He knew the effect he had on her. She was flying back to Houston tonight. That was a promise to herself, but even as she made it, she hoped she had the willpower to live by it.

After they had ordered lobster dinners, he stood to take her hand. "Let's dance," he said, walking inside with her to the dance floor. The restaurant was warmer, the band belting out another blues number. She stepped into Jake's embrace to dance with him, more conscious than ever of the scent of him, the masculine aftershave, the faint, clean soapy smell. His strong neck was warm beneath her fingers, his short hair brushing her hand lightly.

She cared more for Jake than any other man she had ever known. Did she really want to part with him without intimacy? If she did, would she regret it forever? The question continued to disturb her. She had always feared an unplanned pregnancy, a repeat of what had happened to her mother, something she wanted to avoid at all costs. Make love to Jake? Was that so impossible? So fraught with hazard? Birth control was readily available. People made love now with no reason except lust. One night. She wouldn't lose her heart forever over one night with him. A memory to keep—making love with a man she might already be in love with.

The questions badgered her. She desired him, constantly, day and night. His kisses set her ablaze and right now, she wanted to kiss him and be kissed. One night with memories to hold forever.

As if he discerned her thoughts, he tilted up her chin to look into her eyes. "We could go to the hotel suite I've reserved—and eat in private."

"Jake, we have lobster dinners ordered," she whispered, tempted to yield, to take the risk for what she wanted.

"We can get lobster dinners there. Let's eat at the hotel, Caitlin."

Her mouth was dry and she couldn't answer. She merely nodded, her heart pounding. She held his wrist. "Jake, I'm not making a commitment to stay the night."

"I didn't ask you to," he whispered. "Let's go. I'll tell the maître d', pay the bill and he can surprise another couple with free lobsters."

Soon enough, they were back in the limo. As soon as the limo was moving through the quarter, slowly because of the crowd, Jake closed the partition and turned to take her into his arms.

She went swiftly, holding him tightly as she let go all the pent-up desire and poured herself into her kisses. Passion made her hot and eager. She ran her fingers through his hair, combing it back.

Pulling her onto his lap, he cradled her against his shoulder while he kissed her and tangled his hand in her hair to send pins flying. He was aroused, hard against her and his kisses swept her away until his hands were at the neck of her dress, starting to pull her zipper.

While she gripped his wrists, she sat up. "Jake, we've got to walk into the hotel. I won't look presentable."

"You look breathtaking. Every man tonight has turned to look at you. It would be impossible for you to look unpresentable," he whispered, leaning toward her, but she stopped him again.

"How far away is this hotel?"

"Not far. We'll wait to make you happy, but it is definitely difficult. Even more so than when we arrived in the Quarter. You look ready for love, darlin'," he drawled softly, his words pouring over her like warm, sweet honey.

She scooted off his lap, moving away from him slightly while he watched her with a smoldering look that kept her heartbeat racing. She took the rest of the pins from her hair and shook her head, letting the thick auburn locks tumble down on her shoulders.

Finally the limo slowed and stopped. They stepped out beneath a canopied awning in glittering lights to enter a lobby with crystal chandeliers, tall fountains with sparkling water splashing, and an atrium that swept up more than twenty stories. She went with Jake to the desk where they welcomed him.

He had the suite waiting so this was what he had expected to have happen. She was tempted to stop now, but she thought of her earlier arguments with herself.

This night, she would take Jake as a lover, the first man in her life and becoming more important to her each day.

Eight

As Jake held her arm, they took an elevator reserved for the penthouse suite. His pulse pounded. He had the suite reserved for tonight, but he had intended to ask her to go there late tonight after dinner and dancing.

He hadn't planned on how much he wanted her. She had flirted with him, set him on fire with her kisses, given him looks that kept him stirred and hot. When he had suggested leaving for the hotel, he half expected her to flatly refuse for the night.

Instead, he had been surprised, pleased even more by her response and willingness. Seduction tonight became a possibility. The prospect alone aroused him, kept him on edge. In minutes, he would have Caitlin all to himself.

They emerged from the elevator and he ushered her into the penthouse suite and switched on lights. "I'll get champagne to celebrate."

"Celebrate what?" she asked with a slight sharpness in her tone.

"Our friendship," he answered easily, seeing her visibly relax. He shed his coat and tie and crossed the room while she prowled like a cat.

"Jake, this is beautiful and there's already champagne, wine and a huge platter of tempting-looking hors d'oeuvres."

"Help yourself. They spoil me when I stay here."

"You must be a valued customer," she said with a hint of question.

He smiled. "I haven't brought a woman here before."

"Why not?"

He laughed at her question. "This is a private place where I can get away and people don't look here for me."

Caitlin canted a hip to one side and cocked her head to study him. "So why did you bring me, then?"

"Because this is a special night and I wanted to take you to one of my favorite places."

That earned a smile.

"I'll be forever glad you came to my ranch, Caitlin." She was so beautiful she took his breath away. Her hair was silky, thick and soft. As she moved, the slit in her dress revealed her long, shapely legs.

With an effort he walked away to switch on music that he turned low, blues by local artists. He went to the bar to pour two glasses of champagne and picked up the flutes that held the pale bubbly liquid. When he turned, Caitlin was nowhere in sight. Then he saw the door open on the darkened balcony and he walked outside where the night air was still warm.

"Jake, it's beautiful out here," she said. "The view is amazing with the river below us with all the varied boats. I can see the Quarter, even the music carries slightly. What a great place."

"I like it. It relaxes me to be here."

"There, that's how I feel about the house I grew up in. Even more so. I love that place beyond measure. You think of that when you make your decision. Jake, what you intend will involve more than business results. It's people and love and history and roots for me. You'll break my heart if you don't sell to me," she said bluntly.

He lifted his champagne flute. "Caitlin, here's to mending fences between a Santerre and a Benton. You and I can bury that past."

She gazed at him intently without raising her glass. "We can if you cooperate. Otherwise, it may grow worse. But for now," she said solemnly, raising her glass in a toast, "here's to mending fences." And she touched her glass to his with a faint clink.

They both sipped, watching each other. He could see desire plainly in her eyes. She had to see the same in his.

He took her glass and set it on a table beside his and drew her into his arms to dance.

"This is a dream night, Caitlin. I've been thinking about this all week, eager to get home to be with you."

Her perfume was exotic, another temptation. He didn't want to rush her. He wanted to take time, to weave a web of seduction so Caitlin would have the same desires that he did. From her signals, she already did.

His heartbeat raced and he was hot in spite of the pleasant evening temperature. He danced her inside and switched off lights, moving slowly with her, aware of her softness and her sweet smell, her silky hair against his cheek.

The song ended and another began. They continued dancing straight through the momentary silence, into the next song. He wrapped his arms around her, holding her close and dancing slowly with her.

Her soft curves were driving him over an edge. Monday was eons away. He had put it out of mind when he left to pick her up and it crossed his mind only dimly once in the evening. That was tomorrow's worry. Tonight he was with an intoxicating woman. He wanted to hold her, make love with her. He desired her with an intensity that shocked him. He turned to look at her and she gazed up at him, her green eyes sending a lightning bolt of electricity in him. "I want you, Caitlin. I want you to be mine," he whispered.

Jake's words set Caitlin's heart pounding. She was aware of their bodies pressed together, her thighs brushing his as they danced, of her being held close against his muscular chest, his strong arms around her. Seduction was in his every look and move.

For once in her life she was actually contemplating tossing aside her rules and promises and fears. A tremble shook her. Lamplights from the balcony shed a faint glow. She could see lights from boats on the dark, shimmering river, the myriad lights of the Quarter, but she barely noticed any of it as she turned to look at Jake when he drew her closer to kiss her.

She wrapped her arms around his neck and kissed him. They stopped dancing and stood in the semidarkness, kissing while her heart raced. His kiss was deep, possessive, seductive.

His tongue stroked hers, slowly, driving her wild. Lights exploded behind her closed eyelids. His kiss closed out the world. She wanted Jake with a need that consumed her. Never had a kiss stirred the hunger that Jake's kisses did.

While kissing him she clung to him tightly, thrusting her hips against him. How could he do this to her so easily? The question came and then was gone. Her thoughts were on his strong, muscled body, his fiery kisses, and his words, which were tearing away the last barriers around her heart.

In return, she intended to reach his own guarded heart. She hoped to melt him into mush the way he did her.

Jake's fingers were warm at her nape. Continuing to kiss her, he slowly tugged down the zipper to her dress. Cool air washed over her back and shoulders, then lower. Her hands went to the buttons of his shirt to twist them free.

She wanted the obstacles of clothing away, desired him with a need that amazed her. Unfastening his belt, she couldn't control a tremble in her fingers as she hurried. She let her hand drift down over his trousers, feeling his hard shaft. This moment was the last that she could turn back. She gave it a fleeting consideration. It was still possible to stop, to end this and be safe.

He groaned and kissed her, pushing her dress off her shoulders, sliding it over her hips to let it fall around her ankles. Holding his shoulders, she stepped out of the dress and kicked off her shoes.

Jake's hands went to her hips to hold her away and his gaze drifted slowly, taking a thorough perusal that might as well have been his hands on her.

Aching to be back in his embrace, she wanted to kiss him. "Jake," she whispered.

"Shh, Caitlin," he said softly. "Let me look at you. You're gorgeous and I can never get enough." He unfastened her wispy bra and dropped it. His hands drifted down to her lace panties, which he peeled off. His chest expanded as he inhaled.

With deft touches, he peeled down her thigh-high stockings, first one and then the other, his hands caressing her as he removed them.

"Jake," she gasped, each light caress an exquisite torment, fanning fires.

She unzipped his slacks and let them fall, pushing away his low-cut briefs to free him completely. "Jake," she whispered, caressing his thick rod.

He groaned again, pulling her to him and kissing her hard, his warm naked body pressed against hers.

Need was building fiercely as she trailed kisses across his chest and then down his flat belly.

With a gasp he swept her up into his arms. He kissed her as he carried her to a bedroom, placed her on the bed and stretched out beside her. He pulled her into his arms, against his heated body.

"I want you and I want to love you all night long. I want to kiss you from head to toe," he whispered.

Breathless from his words, she kissed him, silencing him, just wanting to love him.

As they kissed, his free hand roamed lightly down her back. When his hand slipped between her upper thighs, she spread her legs slightly to give him access to her.

Tumbling down in an ocean of sensation, she desired him more with each caress. There was no turning back now. She had made her commitment, focusing on loving him, turning loose all caution and restraint.

He shifted to cup her breast with one hand, scooting so he could take the taut bud in his mouth, his tongue circling the tip slowly, driving her wild with need. All Caitlin knew was Jake's hands and mouth and how badly she wanted to make love with him.

His fingers stroked between her thighs, while her hips thrust. She clung to him, suddenly shifting, pushing him down and straddling him to take his thick rod in her hand. She kissed him, her tongue driving him to groan with pleasure, until he pushed her down and pleasured her once again.

He opened her legs, letting his fingers tease and drive her wild and then his tongue followed until she was thrashing beneath his touch, the pressure building. "Jake, love me," she cried, drawing him closer.

Her eyes flew open. "Jake, I'm not protected," she whispered.

He moved off the bed and she watched, drinking in the sight of his bare body, his arousal that declared his desire. He returned to open a packet and put on a condom and then his hands caressed her until he lowered himself and eased into her.

"Caitlin!"

She heard the shock in his voice as he withdrew. She locked her legs around him and held him. "Love me, Jake. I want you now," she cried. "I know what I want."

"You're a virgin," he said, frowning.

She raised up partially to run her tongue over his chest while her hand played between his thighs and her other hand stroked his rod lightly.

As she fell back on the bed, pulling him with her, she met his gaze.

"Love me, Jake, now," she whispered.

He eased into her again, bending his head to kiss her, going slowly. Pain tore at her, bringing a moment of clarity, but it was gone swiftly. Desire had built beyond control or pain. Drawing him closer, she held him as he filled her. He eased carefully, until pain diminished, transforming to pleasure as she moved with him. With slow, deliberate strokes he made love until his control shattered.

Kissing her hard, he held her and pumped faster. She thrashed with him, ecstasy suddenly filling her while she climaxed with a white-hot burst of pleasure.

She cried out his name, unaware of what she had done. Her cries muffled his words as he said her name and endearments until he shuddered, reaching his climax.

She had no idea how long they loved, knowing only that she wanted him more than she had ever dreamed possible. To her surprise, she experienced satisfaction that went beyond any expectations she had.

As they slowed and their breathing gradually became normal she held him tightly. For a moment she hoped she had bound Jake to her in a manner he would never forget her, but then she realized that was an absurd hope. This idyll was a magic spell that held her. She didn't want it to end. Not yet. She held Jake's long, hard body close against her and stroked the back of his head.

Soon he rolled over and took her with him, holding her close with their legs entwined. He gazed at her with worry clouding his blue eyes. "Why didn't you tell me?"

"I don't see why it matters."

"It matters, Caitlin. First of all, I never wanted to hurt you."

She was silent a moment, wondering if he would say the same thing when he told her he was not going to sell her home back to her.

"The hurt was fleeting. Still a little, but not bad."

"It makes our loving special."

"And that's a bad thing?" she asked, feeling disappointment welling up, knowing they were not in love and all he wanted to do was seduce her.

"Not bad, just special, more than I usually am involved in," he said slowly, choosing his words carefully. He looked at her intently. "You're not hurting now?"

"Only slightly," she said, stroking his face. "And it *was* special, Jake."

He pulled her close to kiss her deeply. Her heart now belonged to him. She faced her feelings. She was hopelessly in love with the one man she should have guarded her heart against at all costs. When he released her, she placed her palm on the side of his face, gazing into his blue eyes while he stroked strands of hair away from her face.

"Caitlin, loving you was incredible."

"Even the way it turned out?" she asked.

"Even the way it turned out," he repeated, showering light kisses on her temple and cheek. "Beyond my wildest expectations." He rose up to look at her. "Stay here with me. Let's go back Sunday. I can't let you go now."

"Yes," she whispered, knowing in that moment she was falling in love with a man she not only had intended to avoid falling in love with, but a man she might be furious with in the future. If only he wasn't a Benton. That was a flight of fancy wish because that was the one thing they had between them and the one thing that had brought them together. They had the ranch, past history, old angers and hurts, and now new ones between them.

"You have twisted me around to do what you want," she added softly.

"I think you're the one doing the twisting. It's been worth it." He kissed her lightly again.

Releasing her he slipped out of bed, and leaned down to pick her up. "Let's go to the spa tub."

She wrapped her arms around his neck, momentarily unable to believe what was happening that seemed like a dream. Except the strong arms holding her were real, as real as the hard body she was pressed against.

Jake carried her into an enormous, lavish bathroom with a sunken tub, plants, mirrors and a bearskin rug. Grecian columns graced the decor.

"This is beautiful."

"Absolutely," he said, looking at her and once again, he wasn't talking about the bathroom. He climbed down in the tub, turned on faucets and pulled her close with her back against his chest.

Warm scented water soon filled the tub while he sponged her off and she turned to do the same for him, watching water glisten on his sculpted muscles. "You are one handsome hunk, Jake."

He grinned. "I'm glad you think so, but I believe when it comes to looks, you win, hands down. Speaking of hands down," he said, cupping her breasts with his wet, warm hands.

She gasped with pleasure, closing her eyes as his thumbs began to circle her nipples, so lightly, slowly drawing circles that ignited desire instantly.

"Jake," she whispered, opening her eyes to look at him. He was aroused, his shaft thick and hard. She leaned forward to kiss him as desire burst into flames.

Soon Jake stood and pulled her up with him, water splashing around both of them.

He climbed out of the tub and lifted her up to set her in front of him while he grabbed a towel and began stroking her slowly, drying her.

She clung to his shoulders. "Jake," she said, reaching him to pull him up. "Come here. I want to kiss."

"Shhh, this time we go slowly. I want to pleasure you. I want this to be better."

"Kiss me, Jake. It is better," she whispered, not knowing what she was saying to him and not caring. Desire was hot, an intense need that surprised her because she thought she wouldn't have this driving need again so quickly.

Lifting her in his arms, he carried her to bed and loved her slowly, a sweet torment that built in her until she was trembling. This time when he entered her, pain was fleeting. In seconds pleasure was all she felt, sensations carrying her higher and higher, each stroke building until she plunged into ecstasy, moving rapidly with him as they climaxed together.

"Jake, love me now," she cried. He held her tightly as they arched together, locked in making love. For this moment all was perfect between them. *If only it could last* was a fleeting thought she had. She cried out again in pleasure, rapture enveloping her.

Holding each other, they crashed after the peak. She listened to Jake gasping for breath as much as she was.

Finally, he rolled them both over and combed her hair back from her face while he showered light kisses on her. "Ahh, Caitlin, you're perfect. Marvelous, beyond my wildest dreams. I don't want to leave this bed this weekend. Stay here with me all weekend."

Another invitation. Another decision. Another tie to bind her to him in a manner she had never intended. Yet, how could she say no, given how she felt about him—even stronger now that they'd made love?

I want to stay with him, even if he won't sell my home to me, she realized, the thought scaring her more than the reality. Because I'm falling in love with Jake Benton.

She took a deep breath, then looked into his eyes. "Yes," she whispered, realizing she was taking more chances than ever before in her life.

"Yes, I'll stay the weekend."

He kissed her deeply, another kiss that made her feel special, his woman. A kiss that she hoped wasn't an illusion.

He raised up. "This has been a great night. What I've dreamed about all the past week, but I never knew it would be this stupendous."

"You're insatiable, Jake," she said, smiling at him and he smiled in return, filling her with warmth as they shared this special time between them. If only it held meaning, she couldn't help wishing.

"What are you thinking?" he asked.

"That I wish this could last," she admitted truthfully, watching him to see how he reacted.

"It's going to last for a long time if I have my way," Jake

declared. "I'm not letting you go now that I've found you. Beautiful woman, you don't know what you do to me."

She had to smile, but she wondered if he was even thinking about what he said to her. It couldn't last. Unless…he *had* to sell her the ranch, for intimacy to last between them. Otherwise, how could she stay in his life when he denied her something so important to her?

"I think you're given to exaggeration," she managed to tease, tangling her fingers in his chest hair.

"Not at all. You destroy me. You make me want you all the time. In minutes I'll feel as if we've never made love and want you desperately. You will never know how desperately."

She smiled again at him, running her finger over the tiny stubble beginning to appear on his jaw.

"I stand by what I said about you and exaggeration. But I'm glad you want me and you'll be desperate to love."

"Also, I'm beginning to suffer acute hunger. Since room service takes time, why don't we turn in an order?"

Jake climbed out of bed and she watched him walk across the room and disappear in the living area. Sitting up, she pulled the sheet up beneath her arms to wait. When he returned, he had a towel wrapped around his middle and two thick menus in his hand. He climbed into bed and pulled away her sheet.

"Jake!" She grabbed the sheet, but he gripped her wrists and kissed away her protests and in seconds, as they made love again, menus slipped forgotten to the floor.

It was two hours later when Jake called room service. It had closed for the night, but with a substantial tip promised to the kitchen staff and bellhop, Jake had no trouble placing their orders.

"I'm a loyal customer so they try to keep me happy."

"I'm trying to keep you happy," she said, smiling at him.

"You want to keep me really happy now, you'll come sit in my lap."

She crossed the room to him, wrapped her arms around his neck and kissed him. Jake's arms circled her waist and he held her close as he kissed her in return.

They spent the weekend in the hotel suite until Sunday afternoon when she pulled on her red dress and high-heeled sandals, feeling as if it had been months instead of only a couple of days since she had worn them before.

"Jake, we both have to get back to real life," she said, going to the living area to find him dressed once again in his suit with his phone in hand while he sent a text.

"I know we do," he said. He pocketed the phone and crossed the room to slip an arm around her waist. "Will you go out with me next weekend?"

She gazed into clear blue eyes that held desire even after a weekend of constant loving. She wanted to say yes more than anything. But she couldn't. If he decided not to sell her her family home, her heart would be broken. "Jake, I'm glad that you want to be with me again next weekend. But, let's hold off talking about the future for now. Our relationship is tenuous at best, something unplanned, and impossible to continue if we are poles apart on your decision. This isn't a threat because our relationship isn't that vital." *To you,* she added silently, her heart squeezing. "Anyway," she continued. "I'll see you Monday in Dallas."

"You could go home with me tonight and then you wouldn't have to fly up commercially."

"Thank you, but I already have my ticket, so I should stick to my plans that I've made. We'll know tomorrow where we stand," she added "Unless you can tell me now."

For an instant there was silence between them. A tense

moment when she could hear a grandfather clock tick and nothing else.

Then Jake shook his head. "I still have two men to hear from and then I'll give you an answer. Sorry to put you off so long."

She could read nothing from his expression, so she merely nodded. "Then we better go," she said, picking up her small purse and walking to the door.

Jake gripped her wrist and turned her to face him. He pulled her tightly against him and kissed her, a breathtaking kiss that reminded her of the intimacy they had just shared.

Her heart pounded. Desire ignited again, as hot and strong as before. Longing tore at her and made a knot of her insides. It was a possessive kiss as well as a goodbye kiss. In that moment, she felt certain he was going to refuse to sell to her. She hurt while at the same time, she wanted him more than ever.

Just as she had expected, loving had created new demons for her to fight. She just hoped it created some for him, as well.

She suspected it wouldn't be enough because he had been through all this before and had breakups under his belt. He would move along without much hurt.

She, on the other hand, could be losing her roots, the welfare of people she loved, as well as Jake himself.

She stood on tiptoe and again, poured herself into the kiss, trying to bind him to her by sensuality, the one way to reach him.

He released her, gazing at her intently. "Think about next weekend."

"I'll think about it," she answered, knowing she wouldn't be able to forget his invitation. "We should go now."

He nodded and held her arm as they walked to the limo.

On the flight to Houston, they both were much more silent.

She no longer felt like talking, definitely not like flirting with him. She could feel a chasm opening between them. Maybe it had been there the whole time and hope had blinded her.

At her door he kissed her goodbye again. She watched him walk back to the limo in long strides, climb in and vanish.

With a long sigh she entered her empty condo.

The phone rang and she tossed aside her purse and went to get it. When she answered, she heard Kirby's voice on the line.

"I've been trying to get you," he said, sounding nervous.

Nine

"I was out of town and just walked in the door." From the solemn sound of his voice something had happened and instantly she thought of Cecilia who was getting up in years. "Kirby, is Cecilia all right?"

"She's fine. That's not why I'm calling. Sorry if I scared you about her. Caitlin, Benton Drilling hit oil in that well they're drilling near the house."

Caitlin's insides clenched and she turned cold. "Oh, Kirby," she said, sitting because she felt weak-kneed. "Oh, I hate that. Jake will never sell now."

"Hell, no, he won't. There should be oil right under the house. They'll tear the home place down. I'm sorry to bring the bad news to you, honey, but better from me than from any of the damned Bentons. You still have an appointment on Monday with Jake Benton?"

Hot tears stung her eyes. She had given herself—completely—to Jake. And now, even if he *wanted* to sell to her, he couldn't. It wasn't about her house anymore. It was about business. Money. And the Benton family.

She should have known better.

And he should have, too, she thought. Her blood ran cold for a moment.

"Kirby, when did this happen? When did the Bentons *know?*"

"Saturday morning," Kirby answered grimly. I've been trying to reach you ever since we heard, but your phone just rang and rang."

Oh, no. She'd turned it off so that she and Jake would not be interrupted. And she'd been so deeply involved with him over the weekend that she'd forgotten to turn it back on at all.

"I'm sorry I missed you, Kirby. I still have an appointment tomorrow morning with Jake. I'll call you afterward."

"Sure, honey. Caitlin, don't worry about us. We'll get along and so will you. The old house isn't the world. You don't spend a lot of time in it any longer and it served its purpose well."

Her heart clenched. "I know, Kirby."

"Honey, we love you and don't you worry about us."

"I love all of you, too, Kirby. I'll call you in the morning."

She replaced the handset and gave vent to tears, feeling alone and heartbroken and betrayed as well, although she had only herself to blame for their lovemaking, yet it was not all regrets. She loved him and she had wanted the weekend with him. Oil so close to the house. Jake would want every inch of the land now.

The minute Jake left Caitlin and was back in the limo, he called Gabe. He looked again at the curt text message that simply read: Oil. He had received it Saturday and hadn't read it until Sunday before they left for home.

He tried to get his brother on the phone or by text, but was unsuccessful. He left messages and gave it up until he heard back from Gabriel, but it was obvious they had found oil.

The well was within three miles of Caitlin's house. When he had left town on Friday he had been all set to tell Caitlin no, that he would not sell the land back to her. Then the weekend had happened.

The weekend had been one the greatest. He had to admire her for fighting for those people. She was caring, understanding. They had shared laughter, friendship and easy conversation. She had placed her trust in him and made love when she had known he might not sell. She was the sexiest woman he had known. Thinking about her, he could easily get aroused. Right now if she called him back to bed, he would turn around and go right back to Houston. He wanted her in his bed. He wanted her in his life.

The minute he told her no, she would be gone. She had said as much and he was certain that's exactly what she would do. Friday, he had been prepared to let her go out of his life. Now he wasn't. Each time he thought about telling her goodbye, his insides twisted and a bad feeling swamped him.

"Dammit," he swore aloud, feeling helpless and a loss of control and hating having to sit in the limo without even driving to distract him. He didn't want to tell Caitlin goodbye. Not now.

He mulled over the dilemma and thought of the possibility of offering her a far corner of the Santerre place and moving the house, but there actually were two more men who would report to him in the morning about the possibilities of wind turbines on the ranch and about drilling for oil. Gabe would see him tomorrow. He was certain the decision would be to turn her down.

Tell her no and get over her, he told himself. The prospect was untenable. He didn't want her out of his life. Not yet.

Ten minutes after Jake arrived at his condo, Gabe showed up.

He was casually dressed in Levi's, Western boots and a long-sleeved Western shirt with sleeves rolled up. His dark brown hair was tousled and he had a slight beard as if he had missed a day of shaving.

"Did you get my message?" he asked, following Jake into a living area.

"Yes, I did. So the well came in."

"Yes and a good one," Gabe said, sounding jubilant as he withdrew folded papers out of his back pocket and dropped them on a table for Jake. "Here are figures and information and you can look it all over. I wanted to make sure you knew before you see Caitlin Santerre tomorrow, even though you intend to refuse to sell to her. That old house where she was raised may be in the middle of an oil field. I always told you I thought there was oil on their ranch."

"Well, you were right. We have the mineral rights to the Santerre ranch whether I sell the house or not."

Gabe looked up sharply from the text he was reading on his cell phone.

"You're not changing your mind about selling to her, are you?"

"I'm still debating," Jake said, bracing for the storm that was coming.

"The hell you say. You weren't 'debating' last week." Gabe's blue eyes narrowed. "What did you do this weekend? You didn't answer the text I sent you until Sunday afternoon."

"You didn't answer the one I sent you—period."

"I've been out at the ranch and just got back to Dallas. Where have you been?"

"I was in New Orleans with Caitlin."

Gabriel groaned. "Dammit, did you sleep with her?"

"I don't see that's any of your business," Jake snapped, becoming annoyed with his younger brother's interference.

"Oh, hell. That means you did. That's why you're debating. If you tell her no tomorrow, she won't let you back in bed with her. That's what has you hot and bothered and 'debating.'"

"Gabe, it's none of your damn business what I do with Caitlin and if I decide to sell the land back to her, we still have rights to drill and you know it."

"It would sure as hell complicate things though in a lot of ways. They won't like the trucks, the noise, the drilling. Not to mention if we want to drill close to that shrine of a house she has. Look at the maps I brought you. You're going to let some sentiment interfere with your business sense and a lot of money?"

"There's a lot of land. You know it wouldn't have to be right in that one place."

"Jake, if we're close, it'll be just as bad. What's the deal? You know plenty of good-looking women and you barely know Caitlin Santerre. Dump her and go out with someone else. Someone you know and like."

"Thanks for the keen advice, Mom," Jake remarked dryly.

Gabe leaned forward to place his elbows on his knees and stare at his brother. "She probably slept with you just to get you to sell to her. You sell and she may disappear just as quickly out of your life. Knowing your luck with women, you probably can't even imagine such an event."

"Gabe, you're getting on thin ice," Jake said, trying to hang on to his temper. "Drop the subject of Caitlin."

"I can't believe this. You're letting a Santerre cloud your judgment. After you had already reached a decision about what you would do. She must have been really hot."

Jake stood, his fists clenched, and took a deep breath.

"Look, I'll make a decision and you'll have to live with it, which you can do. Now you're pushing me, Gabe. If I want to sleep with someone, that's my business and selling land back to her is not the end of the world or even a dime out of our pocket. I'll put a steep price on it because she'll pay it, but you stay out of my private life. No more remarks about Caitlin, either."

"I can't believe I'm having this conversation." Gabe leaned back and put his hands behind his head, studying Jake. Jake was angry, fighting it because part of the anger was with himself, part with Gabe, and part with Caitlin for getting him tangled up in her life.

"Want me to tell her?"

"What do you think?" Jake asked.

"Tell her no, Jake. By a month from now, you will have forgotten all about this. You let her keep that land, you'll have nothing but trouble and she could will it back to her half brother."

"She won't do that. There's no love between Will and Caitlin."

"You *care* about her. Damnation, Jake, you *care* about a Santerre. You've hated them all your life. What the hell happened?"

"I got to know her and I like her. I feel sorry for those people who've worked for her grandmother—"

"Oh, no. No, no," Gabe said. "You didn't feel sorry for them last week when you were planning on giving them the boot. Oh, no. That has nothing to do with it and don't tell me it does."

"All right," Jake snapped, his temper rising again. "It's Caitlin. It's land I acquired. The company is drilling on it, but I, personally, bought it and own it, so I can do with it as I damn well please," he told Gabe.

They stared at each other a long, tense moment. Jake

could feel the clash of wills that sparked the air. Then Gabe stood.

"I have to get going. You're right of course. It is your land to do as you please. So we just go from there and see what we can do. In the meantime, we'll make a tidy sum on this well."

"Good deal, Gabe. Thanks for what you've done."

Gabe shook his head. "You're loco, Jake. A Santerre is nothing but trouble. You'll see. She's just using you."

Jake shrugged, curbing the flash of anger he felt. "Time will tell, Gabe."

"Yeah, twenty-four hours of time. Well, it's your choice. You're all grown up now and know what you want to do."

"Thanks for coming by," Jake said.

"Sure. You keep thinking about it. You've had a complete turnaround."

"I'll think about it," Jake said, wondering if there would be a moment when he could let go thinking about it.

Gabe left and Jake closed the door behind him. He picked up the papers Gabe had brought and sat to read them, finding his mind wandering to Caitlin often.

Finally he pushed the papers aside and reached for the phone, wanting to talk to her, missing her and longing to hold her. He released the phone and sat back, thinking about tomorrow. He should tell her no. He had been all set to do so.

She had been a virgin—he was the first man in her life. He felt a mixture of emotions about that. She had to care about him and to have wanted to sleep with him to give up her virginity to him at age twenty-eight.

Had she done it purely to get him to sell to her? He didn't think she had. If he sold to her, would she get out of his life and not want to see him? As a Santerre, would she try to run the drillers off the property?

The logical thing was to refuse to sell and go on with life.

Each time he reached that conclusion, he couldn't face carrying it out. He wasn't any happier with the choice of letting her keep the land because he had looked at the maps Gabe had given him. Her house would more than likely end up in the middle of oil rigs. She wouldn't be happy. By then she might have to move anyway. He should tell her no and he could explain why.

He paced the room restlessly, arguing with himself for another hour before he left to work out and hoped to forget for a few minutes the problems looming in his life.

More than anything, he missed Caitlin and wanted to talk to her.

Monday morning Caitlin dressed with care, trying to look sophisticated, appealing and all business. It hadn't been twenty-four hours since she'd seen Jake but she missed him, missed his company, his kisses, his humor, his flirting, his sexy loving. Today his answer would be no and she had already started doing what she could to find places for Kirby, Cecilia and Altheda.

She hurt because she was in love with Jake, furious with him at the same time, yet she could see from a business standpoint why he would want the old house, buildings, people and animals out of the way. She ached, wanting to be with him. She felt torn in two.

She had rearranged her calendar and booked a hotel room in Dallas since she would be dealing with Realtors over the next couple of days. She intended to spend the afternoon trying to locate a suitable place to move Cecilia and Altheda. Kirby already had job offers from other ranchers. Most likely, Altheda might. They were all comfortably set from the money left to them by her grandmother, but Kirby and Altheda both liked to keep busy.

She pulled on the jacket of her charcoal suit. She wore a matching silk blouse and matching pumps and had her hair pinned on her head. She had already had one call from Cecilia to reassure her to not worry about them. Kirby had received two job offers.

She gazed in the mirror and fought back tears. She was holding on to Cecilia, Kirby and Altheda because they were a substitute family for her—the only one she had. They had been there for her all her life, Kirby teaching her to ride, to care for her horse and later, to develop an eye for a good horse. She couldn't ever let go or lose her love for the three of them and now they were all older with physical problems beginning to be part of their lives. She didn't want them worrying about jobs or income or having to lose each other. Kirby's wife had died ten years earlier. The other two had lost husbands years earlier, before they came to work for her grandmother.

Jake could never understand her close relationship with them because he had a big, close family, even if he did fight with his father on occasion.

She thought about how Jake spent money and the fortune he was giving up because he was too stubborn to do what his father wanted. That didn't bode well for her.

She gave one last look at herself, picked up her briefcase and purse and headed to the airport for her flight to Dallas. She would be in Jake's office in only a few hours. She just wanted to get the meeting over and get away. She was determined to keep control of her emotions because she never wanted Jake to know how deeply she felt for him. Hopefully, after today, all those feelings for him would vanish because it hurt to be torn in two over him.

If he could turn down his father's fortune without hesitation, he could just as easily turn down selling land back to her.

When she landed in Dallas, she rented a car and drove to

Jake's office. Taking a deep breath, she walked into his office after his secretary had announced her.

Jake stood and closed the door behind her. She barely glimpsed a luxurious, spacious office with a balcony, walls of books, leather furnishings, a big-screen television and bar. All she saw was the tall, brown-haired man at the door. His riveting gaze met hers and held. Her heart thudded and her first reaction was to want to walk into his arms and kiss him. He was breathtakingly handsome in a navy suit that made his eyes appear a darker blue.

"Come in and have a seat," he said and his greeting confirmed her guess that he would refuse to sell. His coolness hurt as if nothing had happened between them and the past weekend hadn't existed.

She fought back tears that threatened, determined to avoid letting him see how upset she was over his cold reception. This morning he was all business. She still wondered how much was revenge against the Santerres, driving them totally out of the county and away from him.

Had he seduced her to amuse himself? Or to add his own touch of Benton success over the Santerres?

She sat in a leather chair in front of his desk and crossed her legs. He pulled a chair to face her.

"Let's get this over with, Jake," she said, glad her voice sounded as calm as if she discussed the weather. "Kirby called me as soon as I got home. He had been trying to reach me over the weekend, but of course I didn't take my calls. One more mistake. He told me about the oil. Congratulations to you and Benton Drilling and your brother who predicted this."

"Thanks. My brother is delighted to see that he was right when he said he would find oil."

"That makes your victory over the Santerres so much

arger. You found the oil when my father couldn't. I know you
are not selling back to me."

"Caitlin, would you want to buy the house knowing we're
drilling right by it? With all the machinery, smells, noise and
men working? I've thought about other possibilities. I can get
the house moved."

"I've looked into that. It's a three-story old home—over
a hundred years old. They've told me it would damage it
structurally to move it. There may be a company out there
who will tell me something different, but that possibility
exists. I'm not moving it," she said, mollified slightly that he
was looking at an alternative and trying to work something
out. Maybe he cared more than she had realized. "Maybe
before the past weekend together, but now I want more from
you, a real commitment that you could best show by allowing
me to buy the place." She took a deep breath.

"Caitlin, dammit," he said, placing his elbows on his knees
and gazing intently at her. "That's moving where I'm not ready
to go. I'm offering you hope of saving the house by moving
it. I know what this means to you."

"I'm not surprised, Jake. When you put me off so long,
I figured this was where we were headed. Then when your
brother found oil, I knew the answer. I know you're giving
me the best business answer, the most practical one from your
standpoint. At one point, a compromise of moving it would
have been acceptable. But now I want more from you. More
than you can give me. I don't see any point in discussing it
further." She stood, feeling a sensation of suffocating in his
office that had sunlight streaming through glass, one sliding
glass door open with cool fall air pouring in.

He stood, too. She gazed into darkened blue eyes.

"This isn't what I wanted and this isn't the way I want
things between us to end," he said in a tight voice. He moved
closer to her, placing his hands on her shoulders.

She inhaled, wanting him in spite of her anger and hurt, while at the same time furious with him and wanting him out of her life. "I wish I had never gone to your ranch and tried to get you to sell the land back to me," she said, fighting more than ever to keep from letting tears come. "Get out of my way, Jake. Out of my life. We don't have one thing to say to each other now except you won. The Bentons wiped out the Santerres and you did it single-handedly, seducing a Santerre in your dealings."

That was all their "relationship" had been to him. A game of seduction. And he'd won.

She brushed past him. Before she could reach the door, he caught her, spinning her around to wrap her in his arms. Her protest was destroyed by his mouth covering hers as he kissed her, bending slightly so she had to cling to him.

His tongue thrust deep in a passionate kiss that stormed her senses and brought the weekend swirling back.

The hurt she had experienced all morning skyrocketed. The man she loved was kissing her as if she was totally essential to his life. She wanted him physically, aching for his hands, his kisses and his loving. At the same time, she was enraged with him, wanting to get him out of her life and never see him again no matter how much she hurt in doing so.

He kissed her passionately while one hand caressed her nape, drifting down her back to cup her bottom against his hard arousal.

"No, Jake," she said, twisting out of his arms.

They both gulped for air as they stared at each other. Passion had been hot and desperate.

"Stay out of my life," she said. "I'll get everyone off your ranch and may you enjoy your millions you'll make from the oil discovery."

While her words poured out, she shook with rage and pain.

"Do you really want me to sell it back to you and you and

your people will live in the center of an oil field? Kirby can't run his cattle there. There will be lights and noise and trucks at all hours of the day and night, not to mention the smell. Have you even thought this through?"

"I've thought it all through and faced up to my mistakes in succumbing to your seduction, which I hope to blank out of my memory. Stay away from me, Jake, although I should save my breath. I suspect you have done exactly what you set out to do and you have no further use for me."

"That's damn well not true and you know it. The kiss we just shared makes that plain."

"Get out of my way. We don't have one thing to say to each other now except you won. The Bentons wiped out the Santerres and you did it single-handedly, seducing a Santerre in your dealings," she said, striking out blindly because she hurt.

"Take the time you need," he said gruffly.

"Thank you for your generosity," she couldn't resist replying. "I'm going. You can celebrate your victory, your fortune and one more meaningless seduction. I hope we never see each other again."

She rushed past him wanting to get out while she still had shed no tears. In the elevator, the tears came, blinding her and making her angrier at herself for succumbing to Jake, for falling in love with him, for ever hoping for any concession from a member of the family that had fought with hers for generations.

In the car she tried to gather her wits and get over the emotional upheaval in order to drive to her hotel. Taking deep breaths, she finally got control, wiping away her tears. She tried to shift her thoughts to what to do next.

When she felt she could focus on her driving, she left. Jake had never intended to sell one inch of the ranch back to her and had played her along until he could seduce her and then toss her aside.

She thought of the fiery kiss. Had he hoped for another quick lovemaking in his office? Or that she would let him stay in her life and sleep with him until he tossed her out?

She had no idea what his intentions were, only her own. No matter how badly it hurt, she would get over him. Determined to focus on her problems, she attempted to shove thoughts and memories of Jake out of mind. Jake could live with his conscience now.

The thing she dreaded was telling Cecilia who was an optimist, always hoping for the best and giving everyone the benefit of the doubt. Kirby already expected the inevitable outcome and Altheda was as much a pessimist as Cecilia was an optimist, so she expected the refusal from the start.

As soon as she let them know, she would make her plans, deciding to look into some kind of senior assisted living for Cecilia and Altheda.

The minute she closed the door to her hotel room and was alone, Caitlin gave in to her emotions once more, putting her head in her hands to cry. She loved Jake and she wasn't going to stop loving him any time soon no matter how angry she was with him. His rejection hurt badly and memories were a torment that would only grow worse as she began to miss seeing and talking to him. Had their time together meant even the slightest thing to him? Or had he just been another Benton getting even with a Santerre for past history? Jake hated the Santerres because of his sister. He could easily have done everything in revenge, but it was Will the revenge should have been directed against. Not her. She had been an innocent bystander.

Shocked when she looked at the time, she saw she had cried for an hour. She tried to ignore a pounding headache as she went to the bathroom to wash her face and place a cold cloth on her temple and then at her nape.

She picked up the phone to call Kirby because he would be the easiest call to make of the three. He expected the refusal and had already been thinking about the future.

"Kirby, I'm back at the hotel," Caitlin said, seeing Kirby, probably with his phone while he sat on a bale of hay or perched on a fence.

"He refused, didn't he?"

"Yes, just as you thought he would."

"I don't know why he strung you out, Caitlin. Well, I do know. He wanted to go out with you because you're a beautiful woman now. You probably won't see him again."

"I definitely won't. I told him as much—to stay out of my life."

"Is that what you want?" Kirby asked and she thought she detected curiosity in his tone.

"Definitely. I don't want to see him again," she said, the words hollow and making her hurt more.

"I hope you mean that," Kirby said.

"I'm going to look at assisted living places this afternoon for Cecilia and Altheda. Is there anything I can do for you?"

"Thanks, no. I've had four good job offers. Caitlin, one is down near El Paso. I won't see any of you as often, but I'm thinking about it, because it's a great job."

"Kirby, do what you want. We'll see each other. We don't see each other for months at a time now. Just don't worry about me. I'll be fine."

"I know you will. I'll go check on Cecilia and Altheda and see that they're okay after you break the news. Cecilia is as sentimental about that house as you are. Maybe even more. You'd think she had grown up in it."

"I know. This won't be easy."

"Caitlin, you forget Jake. Go on with your life."

"I will," she said.

"I'll get back with you," Caitlin said and broke the connection. She dreaded telling the women, debating whether to go to the ranch to let them know. Finally she made the call, hurting and crying when Cecilia started to cry. In minutes they concluded the call and Caitlin shed more tears, but she was relieved by Kirby's positive outlook and knew she could count on him to cheer Cecilia and Altheda.

Making a string of calls, Caitlin set up appointments, feeling the only hope for getting over her unhappiness was to immerse herself in work and in getting everyone off the ranch as soon as possible.

Her thoughts shifted to Jake. Was he going out tonight to celebrate with his brother? Or with a woman? How soon would another woman be in his life? For all Caitlin knew, there could have been one in his life all along.

The phone rang. She had told few people where she was staying, giving her cell number to the Realtors. She was surprised to hear her friend's voice. "Ginny, hi. I suppose you called to learn the outcome. It was what I expected."

She received another surprise to hear Ginny say she was in the hotel and wanted to come up and see her.

In minutes Caitlin let her tall, blonde friend into the room. Ginny carried two frosty malts and handed one to Caitlin. The minute she closed the door, Ginny gave her a hug.

"I'm sorry, Caitlin."

"Thanks. Come sit and we'll talk. What are you doing in Dallas? I thought you were at home in Houston."

"I wanted to be with you. I thought you'd need a friend this morning." Worried brown eyes gazed at Caitlin who smiled at her closest friend.

"You're the best. Thanks for the malt."

"You look as if you need it. It was worse than you expected, evidently. When do you have to get everyone off the ranch?"

"There's time. I have one more month. They struck oil and that's that. My house could eventually be in the middle of an oil field. It would be bad even if he sold it back, but he doesn't want to do that, of course. I don't think he ever intended to. I think he was just stalling because he wanted to go out with me."

"You had a good time with him."

"Yes, I did, but now I wish I'd never gone to his ranch. I gained nothing." *Except memories and a broken heart,* she added silently.

"You would have had regrets if you hadn't tried," Ginny said.

"You're right. I would have. If it hadn't been for the oil, I might have had a chance. On the other hand, he's a Benton and he's bitter about Will and his sister."

"I remember that and all the wild stories, that Brittany Benton was carrying Will's baby and he wouldn't marry her. That Will murdered her. That she tried to run him off the road and lost control and was killed. No one will ever really know what happened. I'm sure Will won't ever change his story. He was under oath."

"Will swore to my grandmother that he was telling the truth. He *always* told her the truth. He feared Grandmother."

"He might have feared prison more," Ginny remarked dryly and for a moment was silent. "Will you see Jake again?"

"No. I don't ever want to see him again," Caitlin said and Ginny studied her.

"Caitlin, when I talked to you before you went out with him last weekend, you sounded happy, really happy. Did you fall in love with him?"

Caitlin looked up to meet Ginny's curious stare. "I cared,

but I'll get over it," she said, unable to deny the truth to her closest friend.

"You did fall in love with him," Ginny said. "I knew it. Oh my. That makes everything so much worse."

"Yes, it does, but I'll get over it," she repeated more firmly, wondering how long it would take to stop hurting.

"Next weekend I'll make plans and we'll keep so busy, you won't have time to think about Jake Benton."

Caitlin had to smile. "You do that. I may be busy anyway, trying to get everyone moved."

"All right. Let's see how I can help you get places lined up."

"Ginny, what a friend you are," Caitlin said, feeling slightly better, knowing Ginny would help take her mind off Jake for a while. "I know you're taking time from your work."

"I can do it. I took a few days off. Let's see your list of things to do and what I can help with."

As they went over tasks, Caitlin stared at the phone numbers, scratching out Jake's, recalling this morning and his fiery kiss.

"Caitlin—"

Startled, she looked up and saw Ginny frowning. "I'm sorry, what?"

"You haven't heard anything I've said to you for the last ten minutes. You're worse off than I thought."

Caitlin felt her cheeks burn and hated the blush that caused it. "My mind drifted, sorry."

"Drifted to one Jake Benton. You're really in love with him."

"No, I can't be, Ginny. When I talk to Kirby and Cecilia— no, I'm not," she said, lost again thinking about Jake with a tight knot in her throat.

Was he celebrating now? Was he going to forget her easily and go right on with his life, jubilant with the discovery of oil, never even thinking about what he had done that had been hurtful?

Had their time together meant anything to him?

Ten

Jake had a busy morning. At noon he planned to leave for an hour workout at his condo because he didn't feel like eating lunch. He had made mistakes during the morning—not heard things that were said to him, lost his train of thought in the middle of a meeting and stopped listening several times on business calls.

He had to get a grip on his feelings. Never in his life had he minded a breakup. He had never intended to sell the land back to Caitlin. At first, he had just wanted to go out with her, to make love to her. Then he had liked being with her and he admired her. She became someone he enjoyed, someone who set him ablaze and the mutual attraction had been intense.

He had known it would be bad when he turned her down and he had expected her anger, but never had he thought he would care to this extent. He didn't even understand his own reactions. He'd told women goodbye before. A couple had walked out on him, but it hadn't disturbed him greatly. Or even a little. He had simply moved on.

That wasn't happening this time.

He reminded himself it had only been a few hours since she had walked out of his life, but that shouldn't make any difference. He wanted her back. He missed her. He wanted to look forward to going out with her again. When had she become important to him?

Why had she been so damned unforgiving? He already had the answer to his own question. Those people in the Santerre house were the only people she had. She had no family left except Will and she couldn't count Will Santerre as family. He treated her as if she didn't exist. Jake mulled over her remarks about wanting more now. She had been talking about love, not land or house or money. He drew a deep breath. How important had she become in his life?

As Jake left the building to drive to his condo, Gabe approached.

"I was just coming to see you," Gabe said. "Want to go to lunch? We can talk then."

"I'm going home and for a workout."

Gabe's eyes narrowed. "It must have been bad this morning. You don't skip lunch for exercise. Let's go talk. You can run a little later."

Jake nodded and walked beside his younger brother. They both went to the car in silence that was unbroken until they were seated on the patio of a restaurant.

"All right. You look as if you got kicked by a horse. What happened?"

"Dammit, Gabe. What do you think happened? I wrecked Caitlin's life this week. Well, not hers exactly, but she has to put those people out of the only home they've known for the past—I don't know how many—years. Long before she was born. She loves them because they are the only family she has."

"She can love them on another ranch. Let them move. She's got money and Kirby has a reputation in the area as being the best foreman, bar none. We've got a damned good one, but people say that about Kirby. The man knows horses. They still have two fine horses Kirby bought for them. She'll survive and she'll get over this and so will they."

"Maybe. I still felt like a heel."

Gabe waved his hand. "When trucks get to rumbling across that ranch at all hours, she won't be sorry. I don't think she'll be there much anymore, anyway. She'll forget her anger with you after they get settled into a new place."

"I don't think so, Gabe. That old house means something to her. They've got a month to vacate, but leave it standing until I say otherwise."

"What the hell for?" Gabe asked, studying his brother. "Are you going out with her this weekend?"

Jake had a stabbing pain in his middle. "No," he answered. "I don't know why I let you talk me into this lunch. I'm not hungry and I don't want to talk about it."

Gabe stared at him until Jake looked away. "That's what this is about. You're not angry over having to say no to her. You're undone because she won't go out with you again. You want to see her and she won't agree to it."

Jake clamped his jaw closed and wished he had gone ahead with his exercise and stayed away from Gabe who was making him feel worse.

"Lord, help us," Gabe said. "You're in love with her."

Jake jerked around to look at Gabe sharply. "I am not in love."

"Could fool me. You don't want to eat. You were out of it when you talked to Fred this morning because he told me that he got an answer from you, but that it didn't make sense

Didn't to me, either. I told him to call you back and get it straightened out between you. He said he would this afternoon by two at the latest. Has he already called?"

"I don't remember."

"Damnation, you've fallen in love with her."

"No, I haven't."

"You wouldn't know. You've never really been in love in your life. In love with a Santerre. Jake, that's terrible."

"Thanks for your vote of confidence in this. Get off my back. I'm not in love with Caitlin. I'm not even going to see her again. She doesn't ever want to see me."

"Uh-huh. I'm willing to bet on that one. Unless she was faking interest to get the sale out of you."

"She wasn't faking interest," Jake said, his thoughts more on Caitlin than his conversation with his brother. Was he in love with her? Was this what love was like? This all-consuming need to see and be with someone? "Let's drop this subject because I'm tired of hearing about it."

"Sure, okay by me," Gabe said, switching to talk about a purchase of land they had made in New Mexico.

Relieved to get his mind on something else, Jake tried to focus intently on his brother's conversation only to drift back to thoughts of Caitlin and wishing he would see her after work this week. Was he in love? If he was, what would he do to get over it? How long was the hurt going to last?

By the following week Jake was in a sour mood, quiet at the office, burying himself in work in an effort to shut Caitlin out of his thoughts, but he couldn't do it. He thought about her constantly and he missed her more with each passing day. The empty weekend had been hellish. He had asked someone out Saturday night, hoping to take his mind off Caitlin. Instead, he could barely remember to be courteous and he had ended the evening early. Now he couldn't even remember which woman he had called to go out. To Jake's relief, Gabe hadn't mentioned Caitlin after that first day at lunch.

He missed her, wondered about her and what she was doing. He had reached for his phone to call her repeatedly, each time stopping because there was no point in it and she wouldn't want to talk to him.

Late Thursday afternoon the first week in November, over a week and a half since he had last seen Caitlin, Gabe came by with papers for him to sign.

"You could have sent these over and not brought them yourself," Jake said as he signed them.

"I didn't want you to lose them. I want them signed and back promptly."

"Since when have I lost papers?"

"Since you've been in love with Caitlin Santerre," Gabe snapped. "Where is that Turner contract I sent over Tuesday?"

Startled, Jake stopped signing. "Tracie asked me about that and I told her to find it and get me to sign it. I don't recall hearing from her again."

"Tracie isn't forgetful and you know it. Don't lay this one on her. You've lost it. I can get another contract, because it originates with us. I'll bet it's in your basket or somewhere around your desk."

"I'll get her to look for it," Jake said, making a note. "Then I'll get it to you."

"Jake, you're in a fog and I know it's over Caitlin. Have you called her?"

"No, and it wouldn't do any good to do so."

"Maybe. You don't know until you try. She may be suffering as much as you."

"She's too angry to go out with me."

"Call her and see. You're going to mess up some big business deal if you keep on this way."

"No, I won't," he said, wondering if he could keep his promise. *Call her,* he told himself. He longed to hear her voice.

To his relief Gabe finally left him alone. Jake sat in his empty office with his thoughts on Caitlin. Was he really in love? Should he call her? What did she feel for him? If this was love, under the circumstances, what could he do about it?

For the next four days, he debated with himself whether to call her or not. Finally he decided he would fly to West Texas to look at the new well.

While he was there, he met with Kirby. Then he visited both Cecilia and Altheda. He returned to his ranch, spending a quiet, solitary night thinking about Caitlin and the future. The next day he flew to Houston to go to her office, a public place where she would have to be civil to him.

He learned she was at her gallery. When he drove up to the gallery, which held a bronze statue outside in a landscaped bed, he looked at two black-and-white pictures on easels inside the shop window. One black-and-white was of two small girls. The picture held a bit of whimsy with kites in the background. The girls each had an ice cream cone. Their features were clear and they looked filled with happiness and the innocence of childhood on a summer day. He moved on to the next picture, which was artistic with interesting textures and shapes. It was a building from the French Quarter of New Orleans, he was sure.

Reminding him of time spent with her. Of how he felt about her.

He pulled out his cell and called her.

Caitlin looked up from a ledger on her desk as her cell phone rang. Her pulse jumped when she saw the number. Instantly, anger followed. She was tempted to not even take the call, but curiosity won and she raised the phone to her ear.

"Caitlin." Jake's deep voice was clear. She hated the reaction she had to the sound of his voice. Her pulse raced and she wanted to end the call, but she didn't have the willpower to do so.

"What is it, Jake?"

"I'm in front of your gallery. I want to see you."

Startled, she looked up. She was in her office and couldn't see the large windows out front. "Why? We don't have anything to discuss."

"We might. Do you want to go somewhere or do you have a place where we can talk?"

"Come in, Jake. I'm in my office."

Her heart raced and she glanced down at the blue shirt and slacks she wore. Her hair was in one long braid. It didn't matter how she looked, she reminded herself. Then Maggie, her receptionist, showed Jake into the office and she gazed into his blue eyes, feeling as if she had been struck by a lightning bolt.

Jake wore chinos, a white shirt open at the neck and Western boots. He took her breath and her heart raced and she hated her reaction more than ever.

He glanced around only briefly, gazing intently at her as he closed the door. "Nice gallery and nice pictures in front."

"Have a seat. Why are you here?"

"I want to see you and I want to talk to you." He crossed the room and sat in a chair facing her across her desk. She was happy to keep the desk between them, wanting barriers, hoping to get him out of her office quickly. She didn't want him to know the effect he still had on her and her fury was difficult to keep in check. Beneath the fury was her galloping heart that still melted at the sight of him.

"How've you been?"

"I'm fine. Why are you here?" she repeated, wanting the visit over and done.

"I've been to your ranch to talk to Kirby, Cecilia and Altheda."

Another jolt of surprise hit her. "You have?" she said without thinking, so startled by his statement. "Whatever for?"

"I've hired Kirby to work for me. It seemed a simple solution. He can stay right where he is."

"Kirby agreed to this? And he hasn't even told me?" She stared at Jake in shock.

"He agreed and I asked him to let me tell you. I talked to him yesterday. I went to see Cecilia and Altheda and told them they could stay in the house, that it would not be torn down. It will still be near oil wells and drilling and there will be noise and everything that goes with the drilling, but they can stay where they are."

Stunned, Caitlin sat immobile while she mulled over what he had just told her. "Why did you do this?"

"I want you back in my life," he said. He stood, walking around her desk and her heart thudded as she watched him. She couldn't get her breath. Were his feelings changing? Was he doing this to continue sleeping with her? Or was he feeling something deeper?

"I've been through too much emotionally." He reached to grip her wrist and pull her to her feet. Her pulse raced and questions besieged her.

"Caitlin, I've missed you." He took her wrist again, holding his thumb against her. "Your pulse is racing. We had something great between us and I want you back. I've been miserable without you."

She thrilled to what he was saying and wanted to throw herself into his embrace. At the same time, she couldn't.

"Jake, I have resolutions I've lived by. I tossed them aside that weekend for you. I've missed you terribly—"

"Ah, Caitlin, come here," he said, reaching out again. She pushed his hand away and shook her head.

"I told you when we met that I am not into casual relationships."

"Dammit, this won't be a casual relationship."

"Are you proposing?"

He had been reaching for her again, but with her question, his hand stilled. "I'm not into marriage and you know it."

"While I'm not into a relationship without a binding commitment. Can they stay in the house with that answer from me? Are you doing this to get me back into your bed?"

"It's much more than that. I like being with you. I miss you. I like talking and doing things together. Yes, I want you in my arms in my bed, but I want to be with you, too. Can't we go out together and see where the relationship goes?"

She ached to say yes, but she had spent a lifetime determined to never end up the way her mother had—an affair, an unanticipated pregnancy and the man turning his back on her. While Jake's words thrilled her, she wanted so much more from him.

"Caitlin, if I marry this year, my father will have won his battle," Jake said when she remained silent without answering his question. "My dad will be running my life and he'll continue running it forever. This is a big one. I have strong feelings for you," Jake said and her heart thudded. All her being longed to throw her arms around him, kiss him and forget this conversation, but if she did, she would be more lost than before. And there would be no permanency in her life.

She hurt as if cut by a knife, but now was the time to abide by what she wanted even if it cost her Jake in her life. She would never be happy the other way. It would be fleeting and then she would want more and be more in love with him.

"Jake, your words are magic, but I can't go into a relationship without a commitment. I won't do it, not even after our weekend together."

"Dammit, Caitlin, I love you and I want you," he said, grinding out the words and pulling her into his embrace to kiss her. Unable to resist, she responded, clinging to him and kissing him wildly with all the longing she had suffered over empty, sleepless nights.

"I love you…." Magic words that thrilled her and were another assault against her resistance. She wanted him with all her being, wanted his total commitment forever. She wasn't ever again going through what she had just been through, thinking he was out of her life, seeing their lovemaking turn into memories.

She held him tightly, pouring love, longing into her kisses, running her hands over him, wanting him and aching to lock her door and make love here in the office.

"Go out with me, Caitlin. I've dreamed about you," he whispered, showering kisses on her. "I can't work, I can't sleep, I'm forgetting things I shouldn't, making poor decisions. I want you back in my life. It'll be a commitment."

She looked up at him, framing his face with her hands. "Is that a proposal?"

He looked pained. "You know I will not marry. Dammit, you know why I won't. I refuse to give in to my dad on this because it's a giant, life-changing ultimatum that will make him think he can do the same thing again and again where I'm concerned. No, I can't marry, but I can promise a lasting relationship."

She stepped away from him, trying to gather her wits and her resolve. "If your father told you to forget what he said, whether you marry or not wouldn't matter, would it change how you feel?"

He blinked and looked surprised for a fleeting moment, as

if the prospect had never occurred to him. "I hadn't thought about it that way. And it's pointless to because he's here, in my life and meddling in the worst possible way." Jake's gaze was steady. "I love you, Caitlin."

"I've loved you since before our weekend together," she replied, thrilling to his words that made her want to kiss him, to forget everything else. She clung to fighting for what she wanted.

"If you really love me, you'll marry me," she said. "Don't you see, you're letting him run your life by not marrying if you're really, deeply in love."

"The hell I am. That would be doing just what he wants." Jake walked away, jamming his hands into his pockets, standing in silence with his back to her. She guessed he was thinking about what she had just said and her heart raced.

He turned back to face her, gazing solemnly at her. "Marriage is a giant step, but I've never felt this way before. I'm in love with you. Would you become engaged now and marry me when this year is up? That's not long."

She shook her head. "No. If you truly love me enough to make a binding commitment, then you are allowing his desires to come in the way of our love for each other. I want the marriage, Jake. When we parted, it hurt more than I dreamed possible."

"Caitlin—" he said, taking a step toward her and reaching for her, but she put up her hand. He paused, his eyes narrowing.

"Don't, Jake. I'm sorry. I won't settle for less. You wouldn't want to wait if you were deeply in love with me. At this point in our lives, we both should get over what we feel for each other unless it is one of those loves for eternity that songs are written about. And if it is that kind, we'll know in time because we won't forget or want anyone else. In the meantime,

I think you're allowing your father to control your life and I'm not going into a casual relationship. I refuse to."

"Caitlin, I'm asking for a Saturday night dinner date—"

"No, you're not," she replied quietly. "You want more than that. You want to make love again."

He inhaled and stood staring at her with his fists clenched.

"You don't want that, too?" he asked in a husky voice.

"Yes, I do," she said, seeing him take a deep breath, "but I won't. It hurt, more than you'll ever know, when we parted ways before. I'm not going through that another time. No. I thank you for what you've done for Cecilia, Kirby and Altheda. It will mean a lot to them. I love you, really love you, Jake. Maybe that kind of love that is for a lifetime. While it feels that way now, only time will tell on that one. This is goodbye. I think you will have a bitter, empty victory with your dad."

"You're sure that's what you want?" he asked.

"Yes, I am. Jake, thank you for what you've done for Cecilia and the others."

Nodding, he turned and left, pausing a moment at the door to look at her. Her heart was breaking for a second time over him. She fought the temptation to call him back. He looked at her one last time, then closed the door behind him.

Weak-kneed, she sat down and let tears come, not caring if she was at work. She loved him and he loved her, but not enough to rise above his dad's ultimatum, unless he was simply using that as an excuse. Whichever it was, he wouldn't even offer marriage right now and she had had one weekend of loving without commitment and she never wanted that again because it had meant heartbreak.

Did Jake truly love her? It was a question she would never know the answer to because she was certain he was gone for good this time.

Her thoughts turned to Cecilia, Altheda and Kirby and what Jake had done for the three at the ranch. She wiped her eyes and picked up her phone to call and see if they were truly happy with their new situation.

The house was there. It wasn't hers because Jake didn't sell it to her, but she could go there as long as Cecilia and Altheda lived in it. By the time they were gone, he might have a change of heart and sell that patch of land back to her. The fact that he had taken care of the others made her think his declarations of love might have been heartfelt. Those were not the actions of a man who wasn't in love or had his eye on the dollar. A month ago, Jake would not have agreed to that, much less thought it up himself. He wouldn't have a week ago. Was he really a man in love?

"You did what?" Gabe asked, pacing up and down in front of Jake in the living area of his Dallas condo.

"You heard me," Jake remarked dryly without looking up from an envelope he was addressing. "I've hired Kirby and I'll hire the women at Caitlin's house to work for me. The house stays and they stay and Kirby has two employees who will also go on my payroll and he has cattle that I've bought. In short, only the belongings in the house are Caitlin's. Otherwise, all the rest is mine and my employees."

"You've lost it, Jake. So is she back in your life?"

"Caitlin? No, she's not."

"I don't get this. Why did you hire them then? You don't need them. You didn't want the house to stay. You didn't want those people to stay the last time I talked to you. What the hell happened?"

"I had a change of heart."

Gabe raked his fingers through his thick hair. "I don't get it," he said, repeating himself. "So when are you seeing Caitlin?"

"I'm not. She won't go out with me."

"This gets more complicated. Why won't she go out with you?"

Jake finished and dropped his pen on the desk to lean back in his chair and stretch out his long legs. "She wants marriage."

Gabe snorted. "Well, at least this I understand. You're not a marrying man. This year in particular when you've vowed you won't marry because that's exactly what Dad has told you to do. Well, okay. I'll leave the old house. We have plenty to do where we are right now. Caitlin's out of your life. Who's in?"

"No one at present."

"Ditto here. I've been too busy with work to have a life." He glanced at his watch. "Speaking of, I have an appointment early in the morning. I need to get going now because I have some errands tonight before I go home. See you next week, Jake," Gabe said, picking up a briefcase and hurrying out, closing the door behind him.

Jake stared into space, missing Caitlin, wanting to call her, glad there wasn't a bad feeling between them even if she wouldn't go out with him.

Since he had last seen her at her office, he had thought about what she had said to him. Was he still letting his father run his life, by not marrying? Or was that an excuse? Marriage and commitment had always scared him. He missed her more each day instead of less. He had been surprised by how badly he missed her. It was still as if their weekend of loving had just happened and there was not a growing length of time since then.

He wanted her more by the day. He stood, restlessly pacing the room, feeling alone, wanting her laughter, her warmth, her passion. How deep was his love for her?

He thought about losing her, hearing Cecilia or Kirby someday tell him about Caitlin's wedding.

At the thought, something twisted and hurt inside him. He didn't want Caitlin to fall in love with someone else. Was he really deeply in love, the once-in-a-lifetime kind of love that he didn't think actually ever happened?

He loved her, he wanted her, and he was going to lose her. He swore softly and clenched his fists. Was he letting his father run his life by refusing to marry when he was in love? Was she right about that?

What if his father wasn't in the equation?

For the rest of the night Jake pondered that question, still mulling it over in the morning when he worked out. He finally came to a conclusion.

Eleven

Caitlin placed her camera in her Range Rover and climbed in, turning on the rugged road. She glanced back at the palatial mountain home with a backdrop of spruce and aspen. People stood in the yard and waved to her. She waved in return and then drove around the circle and headed down the mountain to drive back to her home in Santa Fe.

The job had come up suddenly and she was thankful for it because she had been miserable since she had told Jake goodbye. She thought about the pictures of the family she had taken today. It had been a busy, interesting day with some pictures that had pleased her and she hoped when they were finished, her work would please the family.

She inhaled the cool mountain air. It was mid-November now. Snow covered the mountain slopes and she wanted to get to a lower elevation because she didn't want to get caught in any sudden storm.

Two hours later, she turned into the drive of her adobe

house, startled to see a sleek black car parked there. She frowned, wondering who was waiting for her. The car door opened and Jake stepped out.

Her heart missed a beat. She stopped her car beside his and climbed out to face him.

"What are you doing here, Jake? How'd you find me?"

"Cecilia. You always let her know where you are."

"I had a photography job near here. Come inside," she said, turning to go in through the back door. He followed her into the kitchen.

"What brought on this visit?" she asked.

He walked up to her and took her coat off her shoulders, shedding his own jacket and dropping them on a chair before turning back to her.

"I've missed you." Her pulse still raced and his statement kept it galloping. She waited in silence.

"I've thought about what you said. I don't like life without you."

Her resolve slipped a notch. "Jake," she whispered, wanting to reach for him. He looked incredible, exciting, sexy, virile. He had filled her dreams while memories of him tormented her through each waking hour.

"I've given a lot of thought to what you said about my dad controlling my life. Maybe you were right," he continued. She wanted to kiss and hold him, to love him. She trembled and doubled her fists and waited to hear what he had to say and if his stand had changed in the slightest.

Now was not the time to toss aside all her resolutions because she couldn't take another heartbreak. Something had brought him to Santa Fe and she intended to hear him out.

"So," she prompted when he was silent. She held her breath, waiting to see what he would say.

He reached in his pocket and pulled out a ring. "I brought

this for you, Caitlin. Will you marry me? Right away if you want."

"Jake!" She had wanted a proposal, but when he actually asked, she couldn't believe what she was hearing. "You've been so set against it."

"I think you're right. This is what I would do if we pulled my dad out of the equation. I've got to stop thinking about Dad and what he wants me to do or not do. I have to stop reacting to his edicts. It's been pure hell without you. I love you and want you."

His words poured out swiftly as he wrapped his arms around her. She flung hers around his neck, kissing him wildly, joy making her cry. Her heart pounded with happiness while she ran her hands over Jake, wanting him with a consuming need. She twisted free buttons on his shirt, unaware of his hands at her buttons, clothing fell and was tossed away until she was naked in his arms and his hands were everywhere.

Once he paused to run his fingers on her cheek. "Tears, Caitlin?"

"Tears of gladness," she whispered and pulled his head closer to kiss him. In a few more minutes he paused again.

"Bed?" he whispered, picking her up as he kissed her. She twisted free long enough to point. "That way. Turn right," she whispered. "Jake, I've missed you more than you can ever imagine," she said before returning to kisses, running her hands over his shoulders.

"Not half as much as I've wanted you, darlin'. I love you with all my heart, Caitlin. I should have told you sooner, but I didn't recognize it myself. I've never been in love before."

"You know full well that I haven't, either," she whispered and then all words were gone as he kissed her passionately and made love with her.

Hours later she lay in his arms on her bed. She was on her

side, facing him. "Jake, I recall seeing you hold up a ring, but I don't have that ring."

"Damn, I think I dropped it when I kissed you. I'll go find it."

"I'll go with you if I can move. You've demolished me."

"You stay where you are. I'll be right back."

Jake returned, crossing the room to wrap his arm around her.

"Did you find it?" she asked, running her hands over his chest.

He held out the ring. "Darlin', I love you. Will you marry me?"

"Yes," she replied, her heart pounding with joy as she held her hand out to him and watched him slip a sparkling emerald-cut diamond on her finger.

"Jake, the ring is gorgeous," she said. "It's huge."

"So is my love."

She kissed him and he carried her to bed to make love again.

It was in the early hours of the morning when she was in his arms. A small light burned and she held her hand out to admire her new ring. "Jake, I love my ring. And I love you."

"Good. And I love you, too. I want to marry soon."

"What's soon?" she asked, thinking of jobs she had booked in the next few months.

"Tomorrow would be nice."

"Tomorrow!" she said, laughing. "How about a Christmas wedding?"

"Sounds good. But the sooner the better. And then a long, long honeymoon afterward."

She laughed. "What about your parents?"

"I'd be lying if I told you they will welcome you, but I think they'll adjust and when they get to know you, they will love you, too."

"I hope. We've had enough dissension in my family."

"Would you consider marrying in Dallas?"

She thought about it. "That would be fine. Houston is not that far away."

"Great. We'll have a lot of people."

"I can imagine," she remarked. "I can tell you who we will not have."

Jake looked into her eyes. "Your half brother."

"That's right, Jake. I think I've seen and heard the last of Will because he wouldn't attend our wedding if I asked him."

"Do you care?"

She shook her head. "Sadly, no. I don't miss him at all. He'll never come back here and he won't acknowledge that I'm related to him."

"If you don't care, then I can tell you, I'm glad he won't be here. I would find it really difficult to welcome him to my wedding."

"I understand. No problem there."

"Now, we've discussed Will. Let's close the door on that one. I don't want even a discussion about him to put a damper on tonight or any other time between us."

"Impossible," she said, smiling at him. "I'll look at my ring and think about my handsome hunk of a husband-to-be and the wedding we'll have. What else is there? If you can't get him out of mind, then I'll have to do something to take your thoughts elsewhere." She smiled at Jake.

He rolled over. "For a woman who was a virgin, pure and sweet only a short time ago, you are a wanton sex kitten."

"Kitten? That's not good," she said, rolling again on top of him. "Tigress, now that would be a good description. I'll have to earn that one," she said and kissed him. As his arms closed around her to hold her tightly, she was swept away by passion.

Twelve

The second weekend in December Caitlin stood in the lobby waiting to walk down the aisle. Dressed in white silk, she was on Kirby's arm. Cecilia and Altheda were seated where her grandmother would have been.

"Kirby, thank you for doing this," she said, looking at the man she had known all her life. Dressed in a tux, his weathered skin was still deeply tan even though it was winter. His brown hair was thick with gray strands. He smiled at her.

"Caitlin, I just wish your grandmother Madeline could see you. She loved you from the moment you came into this world. She always said your dad made the mistake of his life by not raising you, but it was the blessing of her life that he didn't."

"I miss her. I loved her with all my heart."

"Jake's a good man, Cait. He'll be good to you. He did right by all of us."

"That he did and I think he's a good man. So are you."

"It's time to start now," the wedding coordinator said, kneeling to smooth Caitlin's train that was spread behind her.

Caitlin and Kirby began the walk down the aisle. When she looked at Jake, he smiled and her heart beat with happiness. She loved her handsome husband and now she would be married to him. Someday she would have her own family, hopefully soon, because she wanted elderly Cecilia and Altheda to know her children.

She forgot everything else as she drew closer to Jake and looked into his blue eyes that were filled with love.

They said vows and prayers, he kissed her and finally they were introduced to guests as Mr. and Mrs. Jacob Benton.

When they walked back up the aisle, she paused to hand roses to Cecilia and Altheda. She smiled at Jake's parents and received only a faint smile from his mother and a flat stare from his father. Walking with Jake, she laughed with joy. "I can't believe I'm a Benton now."

"You are definitely a Benton now and forever," Jake said, smiling at her.

It took another hour for pictures before they could get to the country club for the reception.

When toasts were given, Gabe stood up and raised his champagne flute high. "A toast to Caitlin and Jake, who have helped bring a beginning to the end of a family feud that started with the first Bentons and Santerres to settle in Texas. A toast to them for bringing peace to two families, and a wish for a wonderful future filled with love for them."

Jake looked at Caitlin and smiled as he hugged her lightly. "No feud between this Benton and Santerre. Far from it."

She laughed. "Absolutely, love."

Later in the afternoon, Jake stood with his brother and friends. "Okay, Jake," Nick said, grinning. "You didn't keep your part of our pact to avoid marriage. Now you have to put a million in the pot because you've definitely lost the bet and Tony is our winner."

"Thank you, guys. The pot is welcome."

"At least both of you are happily married and not pushed into something you didn't want to do," Tony said. "I told you I would outlast you."

"I knew I'd outlast all of you," Gabe said.

"Only because you're younger."

"And more leery of marriage than anyone. Our dad will be on you now about it," Jake said.

"He thinks I'm too young. He's told me," Gabe stated with a grin. "I agreed absolutely, so we're both happy. But now I don't get that giant inheritance all to myself. You can well afford to lose this bet with Tony and Nick because you are back in Dad's good graces. Someday you'll be enormously wealthy. I couldn't imagine you holding out until the year was up."

"I could," Nick remarked dryly. "Jake can be stubborn as a mule."

"Well, I hadn't planned on Caitlin coming into my life." He turned to Tony.

"Okay, Tony, so what will you do with the money you've won?"

"First, I'll have a party. Gabe, you're invited even if you didn't participate in the bet. I'll find a fun place for a weekend. Nick, can you and Jake tear yourselves away from your wives?"

Jake glanced across the room at Caitlin.

"Never mind. I'll find something where the wives can come," Tony said.

"You'll have more fun if they're there," Nick said.

"You mean *you'll* have more fun," Gabe said, laughing. "Thanks for including me."

"You've always been a tag-along, you might as well continue," Tony said and the others laughed.

"I think I've been away from my bride long enough," Jake said, excusing himself and moving away from his friends to get Caitlin to dance.

"This is the only way I can get close to you," he said, holding her in his arms and dancing to a ballad.

"I thought you'd never come back."

"I'll always come back," he said. "I figure about one more hour here and then we're gone."

She smiled at him. "It's wonderful, Jake. It's a dream come true in my life."

"It is for me," he said solemnly. "It scares me when I think how close I came to losing you."

"Not really," she said. "I don't think you could have ever lost me. I was so in love with you."

"I want you to show me. I'm not sure I can wait that hour."

"Yes, you can and we will," she said, bubbling with joy. "I have to be married to the most handsome man in the world. You look wonderful, Jake."

He smiled at her. "I'm glad you think so. I believe you're a bit biased. While I, on the other hand, am coolly objective when I look around and then tell you that you are definitely the most beautiful woman ever."

She laughed with him.

"Ah, Caitlin, I will never forget that first moment I saw you on my porch and couldn't believe my eyes. A beautiful woman, mysterious, unexpected, waiting on my porch. My life has never been the same since."

"It never will be again," she said, smiling up at him. "I'll always remember that moment, too, when you stepped out and we looked into each other's eyes. Maybe I fell in love right then."

"I'm the one that did the falling in love then. I just didn't know it. So here we are—starting a life together."

"We have a lot of friends here. I've enjoyed getting to know Nick's wife, Grace. When we get back from our honeymoon, we're getting together with them. She had Michael and Emily with her for a few minutes at my shower before they were picked up by her aunt. Michael is an adorable little boy who looks just like Nick. Emily looks a little like him."

"Only Michael isn't Nick's baby. Michael's biological father was Nick's brother who died shortly after Michael was born. He never saw Michael and never married Michael's mother who also died shortly after Michael's birth," Jake said.

"That's sad, but Nick and Grace love him as if he's their own."

"He is their own in every way and he does look like Nick."

"Emily is really precious."

"You're showing a high interest in babies. Cool it until I've had a few months of having you all to myself."

"Of course, just someday in the not-too-far-distant future—"

"I know and I agree," he said. "Right now, I have other plans."

"One more hour."

"I'll try," he said as the music changed to a fast number and she moved out of his arms to dance.

It was over two hours when Jake finally held her hand and they rushed to the waiting limousine to be whisked away to Jake's private jet.

After a stop in New York for three days, they flew to Switzerland for their honeymoon, moving into a chalet Jake had leased.

The view of snow-covered mountains was breathtaking, bu

her attention was captured more by her handsome husband as he pulled her into his embrace.

"At last, I have you all to myself and we are going nowhere for days."

"I feel the same," she said, wrapping her arms around his neck. He kissed her and she closed her eyes, standing on tiptoe, holding him, feeling his heart beating with hers. "I love you, Caitlin," he whispered and returned to kissing her.

Joy filled her and she kissed him passionately, certain her life would be filled with happiness with Jake. She already loved him with all her heart, unable to imagine life without him. "That family feud just died completely, Jake," she whispered. "I intend to seduce a Benton tonight and make mad, passionate love and there will never be bad moves between the Santerres and the Bentons again."

"Absolutely not. Love, sexy love. Let me show you," he said, his head dipping down as he showered kisses on her and began to unfasten her buttons.

"I have to be the happiest woman on earth," she whispered, certain it was so, holding him close to her heart and knowing he would be there for all her life.

* * * * *

COMING NEXT MONTH

Available June 14, 2011

#2089 THE PROPOSAL
Brenda Jackson
The Westmorelands

#2090 ACQUIRED: THE CEO'S SMALL-TOWN BRIDE
Catherine Mann
The Takeover

#2091 HER LITTLE SECRET, HIS HIDDEN HEIR
Heidi Betts
Billionaires and Babies

#2092 THE BILLIONAIRE'S BEDSIDE MANNER
Robyn Grady

#2093 AT HIS MAJESTY'S CONVENIENCE
Jennifer Lewis
Royal Rebels

#2094 MEDDLING WITH A MILLIONAIRE
Cat Schield

Harlequin® Blaze™ brings you
New York Times *and* USA TODAY *bestselling author*
Vicki Lewis Thompson with three new steamy titles
from the bestselling miniseries SONS OF CHANCE

Chance isn't just the last name of these rugged
Wyoming cowboys—it's their motto, too!

Read on for a sneak peek at the first title,
SHOULD'VE BEEN A COWBOY

Available June 2011 only from Harlequin® Blaze™.

"THANKS FOR NOT TURNING ON THE LIGHTS," Tyler said. "I'm a mess."

"Not in my book." Even in low light, Alex had a good view of her yellow shirt plastered to her body. It was all he could do not to reach for her, mud and all. But the next move needed to be hers, not his.

She slicked her wet hair back and squeezed some water out of the ends as she glanced upward. "I like the sound of the rain on a tin roof."

"Me, too."

She met his gaze briefly and looked away. "Where's the sink?"

"At the far end, beyond the last stall."

Tyler's running shoes squished as she walked down the aisle between the rows of stalls. She glanced sideways at Alex. "So how much of a cowboy are you these days? Do you ride the range and stuff?"

"I ride." He liked being able to say that. "Why?"

"Just wondered. Last summer, you were still a city boy. You even told me you weren't the cowboy type, but you're...different now."

He wasn't sure if that was a good thing or a bad thing. Maybe she preferred city boys to cowboys. "How am I different?"

"Well, you dress differently, and your hair's a little longer. Your face seems a little more chiseled, but maybe that's because of your hair. Also, there's something else, something harder to define, an attitude…"

"Are you saying I have an attitude?"

"Not in a bad way. It's more like a quiet confidence."

He was flattered, but still he had to laugh. "I just admitted a while ago that I have all kinds of doubts about this event tomorrow. That doesn't seem like quiet confidence to me."

"This isn't about your job, it's about…your…" She took a deep breath. "It's about your sex appeal, okay? I have no business talking about it, because it will only make me want to do things I shouldn't do." She started toward the end of the barn. "Now, where's that sink? We need to get cleaned up and go back to the house. Dinner is probably ready, and I—"

He spun her around and pulled her into his arms, mud and all. "Let's do those things." Then he kissed her, knowing that she would kiss him back, knowing that this time he would take that kiss where he wanted it to go. And she would let him.

Follow Tyler and Alex's wild adventures in
SHOULD'VE BEEN A COWBOY
Available June 2011 only from Harlequin® Blaze™
wherever books are sold.